Yosl Bergner's Last Dreams

ABOVE ALL YOSL Bergner was a great painter. "Audrey is the artist," he used to say, "but I am a painter." By which he meant that his wife was gifted, whereas he was more of an artisan. All his paintings told stories. In life, too, he was a great storyteller. And he loved to read; Dostoyevsky and Kafka being particular favourites. What stopped him becoming a writer himself was the shadow his father cast over the typewriter. Melech Ravitch was one of the foremost Yiddish poets of the interwar years. The very first story I wrote – Uncle Vlad – featured a family feasting on living butterflies. Years later I discovered that Yosl Bergner had – coincidentally – produced a canvas that matched my vision. Visiting Israel towards the end of 1978 I sought him out, and visited his famous studio on Tel Aviv's Bilu Street for the first time. It was the beginning of our friendship, and (in a manner of speaking) our collaboration. Yosl loved to tell me his dreams, the more outrageous the better, in the hope that I would incorporate them in one of my stories. Oftentimes I did. What follows are Yosl's final dreams, a few of which are indeed incorporated in this collection.

Yosl awakens – in his dream – to discover that his penis

has grown longer, and that it is still growing. In fact it grows so long that it leaves the house and slithers along the pavement. Yosl chases after it, but try as he might he cannot catch it. He begins to worry that people will notice, and wonders how he might conceal it. He looks around. There is a small window. On the other side of the glass two women are watching. "Kafkaesque," says Yosl, when he concludes the retelling. "No," I say, "more like one of your paintings."

Yosl is carrying a painting that consists of stones, one balanced upon another. The problem is that the stones are not painted, but real. Yosl struggles to hold them all together, but is unable to stop some falling out. He wants to pick them up, but he has to keep balancing the remaining stones. "Guess who helped me?" says Yosl. I cannot. "Einstein," he says.

Yosl has a beautiful dream. I must remember this, he thinks (in his dream). But when he awakens he forgets it immediately. He goes back to sleep in hopes of re-entering that lost domain. In his new dream he encounters a group of people. "Who are you?" he says. "Who are we? Why, we are the people from the dream you forgot."

Yosl has no underpants. Someone tells him there's a pair at the top of the building. It is one hundred stories high. He runs up the stairs. In a room at the top he finds the underpants. He attempts to pull them on, but they do not fit. They are women's underpants. Long ones. The true owner bursts into the room crying, "Take off those underpants, they belong to me." Yosl replies: "I cannot take off what I cannot get on." She says: "They are mine."

Yosl stands before a large palace in the Roman style. "I don't like it," he says. "But you built it," says another. "My mind is made up," says Yosl. Whereupon the palace collapses on his head and kills him.

Yosl goes to sleep thinking, "I must dream a dream for Clive." But as soon as the dream begins a voice warns him: "Stop the dream. It will be a nightmare. Believe me." "Can you believe it?" says Yosl. "The dream tells me to stop dreaming. And of course I do."

Yosl is on his knees trying to clear a floor covered with the number 7, which he hates, determined to replace them with the number 8. But no sooner is his back turned than the 7s take over again. "What have I got against 7?" says Yosl. "Perhaps because 7 is connected with death, as in shiva," I say, "whereas 8 is more buxom, more life-affirming."

On Friday January 6 2017 I telephone Yosl and Audrey, as I do every Friday. The conversations with Yosl have become one-sided, since he refuses to wear a hearing aid. He says he is tired, and has no new dreams for me.

On Friday January 13 Audrey tells me that Yosl has deteriorated over the last few days, and no longer goes daily to the studio. In fact he has withdrawn to his room upstairs. Audrey carries the phone to him. I hear her calling, "Yosl, Yosl," without response. I begin to fear the worst. But eventually there is a response. "It's Clive," says Audrey. Yosl starts to speak: "I've been thinking about your beautiful voice." At first I think he is being funny, but then I realize he thinks I am someone else. "It's Clive Sinclair," says Audrey. "Clive Sinclair," says Yosl, not really knowing who that might be. They are the last words I hear him speak.

On Tuesday January 17 I call Audrey. She tells me that Yosl's world is now his room. Hinde, their daughter, has set up a TV for him there, but once in the chair he dozes. Ardon, the family doctor, has been to see him. "There is nothing wrong with him except age," he concludes. Yosl is 96. "He could go tomorrow, or in a few weeks."

The following day a friend – who works for Reuters in Jerusalem – repeats an unconfirmed report that Yosl has died. As soon as the story is authenticated I call Audrey. She tells me that over the weekend Yosl would cry in the night, "I want to die". She didn't believe him. But this morning two helpers went upstairs to wash Yosl. Afterwards he suddenly slumped forward in his chair and was gone.

Perchance to dream.

SHYLOCK MUST DIE

Also by Clive Sinclair

Novels

Bibliosexuality

Blood Libels

Cosmetic Effects

Augustus Rex

Meet the Wife

Short Stories

Hearts of Gold

Bedbugs

For Good or Evil: Collected Stories

The Lady with the Laptop

Death & Texas

Travel

Diaspora Blues: A Personal View of Israel

Clive Sinclair's True Tales of the Wild West

Essays

A Soap Opera From Hell

True Crit: On Westerns & the West (with Seth B Sinclair)

Biography

The Brothers Singer

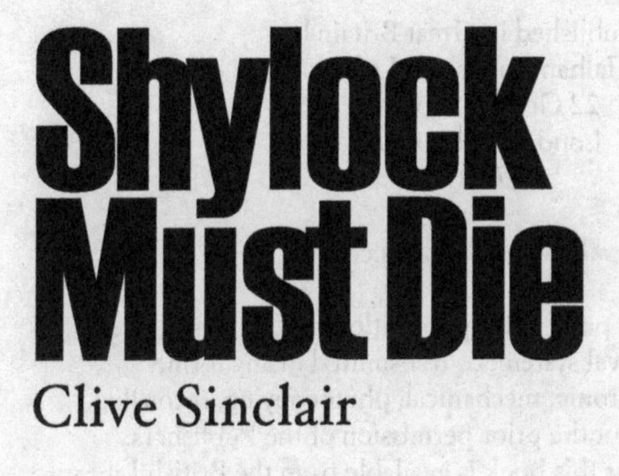
Shylock
Must Die
Clive Sinclair

ph
HALBAN
LONDON

First published in Great Britain by
Halban Publishers Ltd.
22 Golden Square
London W1F 9JW
2018

www.halbanpublishers.com

A CIP catalogue record for this book is available from the British Library.

ISBN 978-1-905559-94-7

Typeset by AB, Cambridgeshire

Printed in Great Britain by
CPI Group (UK) Ltd, Croydon CR0 4YY

Acknowledgements

"Shylock Must Die" was first published in *Death & Texas*. "A Wilderness of Monkeys" was written as a result of a three-week stay in Venice at the invitation of Professor Shaul Bassi for an Anthology inspired by the 500th anniversary of the Venetian Ghetto. Thanks are also due to Phillip Davis, editor of *The Reader*, where "Shylock's Ghost" first appeared. The author would also like to acknowledge the continuing support of the following: Murray & Sheila Baumgarten, Yosl & Audrey Bergner, Pamela & Jonathan Lubell, Judy Stewart. Further thanks are due to Yosl Bergner for granting permission to use his powerful image on the book jacket.

For Seth & Haidee

CLAUDIUS:

'Tis sweet and commendable in your nature, Hamlet,
To give these mourning duties to your father.
But you must know your father lost a father,
That father lost, lost his, and the survivor bound
In filial obligation for some term
To do obsequious sorrow.

Hamlet: Act 1, Scene 2

Contents

SHYLOCK MUST DIE 1
TEARS OF THE GIRAFFE 41
A WILDERNESS OF MONKEYS 59
IF YOU TICKLE US 87
SHYLOCK OUR CONTEMPORARY 115
AIN'T THAT THE TRUTH 139
SHYLOCK'S GHOST 165

SHYLOCK MUST DIE

WHEN MARCO POLO sailed home from the East, he returned with many novelties. Among them were manuscripts written in unreadable pictograms on strips of palm leaf. Each strip was about a metre in length, and as wide as a thumb from tip to base. They were bound together by cord, which was threaded through holes on either end of the leaves. On the top and the bottom were thicker slats of wood, which served as protective covers.

As soon as merchants began to trade with China, they brought back many more of these manuscripts, some twice the size of Polo's originals. Poor Venetians hung these impenetrable stories on their walls in place of tapestries. My father had a brighter idea: he hung his over the windows. Later he devised a way of altering the angle of the leaves, so that he could control the amount of light that entered his office. He liked the chiaroscuro effect that this created. It resembled life, he said, in which some things are revealed and others hidden. He called his invention a Venetian blind. When friends asked him how they too could make a Venetian blind his answer was always the same: You poke his eyes out.

"As far as our family is concerned," he said to me, "the

more blind Venetians the better." He made his living by seeing what they could not see, by penetrating darkness and mysteries on their behalf. He was their private eye.

When I was nineteen he passed on one of his cases to me. He said it would be easy, and would provide an instructive introduction to the profession.

It is a commonplace that a man never forgets his first time with a woman. I remember my first client in the same way. Signora X was not a beauty, but I retain the image of her sitting in my office in the late afternoon. It hangs in my memory like a portrait by Titian. The sun squinted through the blinds my father had fashioned, and transformed her body into a staircase of light, which my impolite eyes ascended. I vowed inwardly to defend her against all enemies. The foremost of whom turned out to be her husband.

She told a sad tale of betrayal and obstinacy, while tears slithered down her cheeks like glass snails (an effusion she ascribed to the sun). In short she had married a pig. Of course he did not regard himself as such. On the contrary, he thought of himself as a pious Jew. He did not beat her, but every morning after prayers, he cursed God for giving him such a shrewish wife. He claimed that was why he no longer lay with her. But she was convinced that he was keeping a mistress somewhere in the Ghetto. She confronted him with her suspicions, which he did not deny, and yet he refused to offer her a divorce, to grant her the infamous *get*, without which she would be unable to remarry. In despair she commissioned me to find irrefutable proof of his infidelity.

I laughed when I set eyes upon this Romeo. He was as bald as a ball of mozzarella. It seemed to me that he was lucky to have found a wife, let alone a mistress. But he did have one. And to prove it was childishly simple. The cleric I chose as my witness was Rabbi Leone Modena. We stood together beneath the woman's casement, which she made no attempt to shutter, and watched as she entertained my client's unfaithful spouse. He turned out to have as little backbone as he had hair. When confronted by the rabbinical authorities he burst into tears. His wife got her *get*. I believe she has since remarried. My father congratulated me on the success of my initial investigation, but cautioned me against over-confidence. Of course I did not heed his advice, and came to bitterly regret it.

****

My next client was none other than Rabbi Leone Modena himself, a man of wisdom, and some ten years my senior. He had been impressed, he said, by the exemplary discretion I had shown in my dealings with Signora X. He took a seat. The light wrapped itself around him like a prayer shawl.

"Imagine me a Sicilian ruffian," he said, "quite prepared to cut out your tongue if you should gossip about his predicament."

I replied that such imaginings were redundant, since the code of my profession counted the office of a private eye on a par with the confessional of a priest.

"Are there many private eyes in Italy?" said the Rabbi.

"At least two," I said. "Tubal Sr and his son. To the best of my knowledge."

"My predicament is this," said the Rabbi: "I owe money to a loan shark. You are thinking such a creature is as kosher as a lobster. But to whom else could I turn? To a member of my congregation? Usurers are always Jews, loan sharks are anything but. This was their advantage to me. But they have drawbacks too: usurers are talmudic in their appreciation of contractual obligations, whereas loan sharks favour muscle and steel. One is hated, the other is both hated and feared. And I am greatly afeared."

I asked the obvious question: "Why did you need the money?"

"I have a weakness, which my wife calls an addiction," said the Rabbi. "I am a gambler. But a very poor one, alas, and my losses multiplied. Thanks to the loan shark I have paid off those creditors. Only to find myself in deeper waters. The loan shark has bigger appetites, which I cannot satisfy. Last week his myrmidons took my son – the apple of my eye – and threatened that I would not see him again unless I cleared my debt – which increases by the hour – within the week."

"The loan shark is acting outside the law," I said, "why not report him to the authorities."

The Rabbi laughed: "I should report him to himself?"

"Can you meet his demands?" I said.

"Only thanks to Shylock," he said. "He is one of us. His profession may stink like yesterday's fish, but he is a mensch."

"What do you want of me?" I said.

"To help redeem my first born," said Rabbi Leone Modena.

Two nights later we met again by the Ghetto's locked gate, and bribed the guard to let us trespass. Calle Vallaresso, our destination, was full of gambling dens, out of which rakes and prostitutes tumbled like dice. Our rendez-vous was at its darker end, deserted and dead-quiet, save for the sound of the water gently slapping the banks of the stinking canal.

"Young Tubal," said the Rabbi as we waited, "you must prepare yourself for a shock. After I collected the money from Shylock, I begged the Eternal One for the strength to resist temptation. But in his wisdom he turned a deaf ear."

"How much remains?" I said.

"About half of what is needed," he said.

"In which case your boy is in grave danger," I said.

"I trust that the Almighty will spare my son, as he did Isaac," said the Rabbi, "perhaps with your assistance."

Out of the darkness three figures emerged; two men nearing thirty, flanking a boy not yet thirteen: Zebulum. The man on the right was holding a lantern, which paved the canal with cobbles of gold. Because they were dealing with Jews they did not bother to hide their faces.

"Here is your boy," said the man with the lantern. "Where is the money?"

"Here is one half," I said.

"And the other?" said the man with the lantern.

"You will have that tomorrow," I said, handing over the satchel.

"Antonio," said the man without the lantern, "these Jews take us for fools."

So saying he silently slipped a stiletto from its scabbard and sliced open the boy's belly, as if he were a trout. I will not describe the Rabbi's lamentations, which I hope one day to forget.

"Bassanio," said his partner, "what have you done?"

"I have taught the Christ-killers a lesson," said the murderer. "For half the money they get the boy, but drained of blood; that is forfeit, for this earthly and that other eternal debt."

Shylock, on the other hand, immediately wrote off the ducats he had advanced the Rabbi. "What," he said, "I should slaughter another of his chicks?"

From time to time I heard of Rabbi Leone Modena, who had become a wanderer; some claimed that they had seen him play the fiddle at a wedding, others that they had seen him preach a sermon. Some claimed to have read books that he had written, among them an autobiography, and a polemic against gambling. Readers may have been converted, but not the writer: he gambled away his daughters' dowries. There were rumours that his wife had gone mad. "If tragedy strikes, if fortune turns ill," he was reported to have said, "What can I do? Let me imagine I lost it at play."

I could never forgive myself for what happened to the Rabbi's boy, though I did not know what I could have done to prevent the butchery. But if only I had done something, I would not have felt so bad. The murderer acted with impunity, because he guessed – correctly – that the Rabbi's bodyguard was unarmed. So I took to carrying a dagger. The weapon sent out a message: If you prick us, you too will bleed.

****

Years passed. I was no longer Young Tubal, but Tubal proper. I married, and – thank God – we had sons. Others, like Shylock, were not so fortunate. Near my father's age, he was blessed with only one child, a daughter, before his beloved wife, Leah, had been taken from him. She died of the influenza. If she had lived she might have saved him from the folly that destroyed his good name. But she was not spared.

It began one Saturday, after services in the synagogue.

"Shabbat shalom, Shylock," I said, kissing his cheek.

He looked me in the eye. "Business is good, is it not, Tubal?" he said.

I nodded: "Sinners are never in short supply."

"In which case you will have no problem in lending me three thousand ducats," he said.

"Has the world turned upside-down?" I said. "Have lenders all become borrowers?"

"I have such a scheme, Tubal," he said, "that should it come to pass will make good an ancient grudge. But to finance it I need not credit, which I have in plenty, but gold to raise up the gross." Seeing that I was not yet convinced he added: "It will be an act of healing, a tikkun olam."

"The Ghetto is full of usurers," I said, "why have you come to me?"

"Because you are one of those who suffered the wound," he said, "one of those who are not yet fully healed."

Then he told me his plan.

"You are familiar with Antonio, of course," said Shylock, pacing back and forth, "that honourable man, that saint among merchants. When I pass that paragon on the Rialto I always step aside, to evade his phlegm, or the kicks he aims to clear unclean dogs like me from his path. But yesterday was different: in place of kicks there were handshakes. It was as if I had suddenly become human in his eyes. Of course there was a reason: he needed three thousand ducats. His best-beloved Bassanio is to go a-courting, and must fit out a ship. I agreed, Tubal, I agreed. Said that I only wanted his friendship, and his love. Said that I would let him have it without a minim of interest. Then I said, as if in jest, that all I required, should the bond become forfeit, was a pound of his flesh."

I said that he was mad, and that I would not advance him so much as a ducat.

"Listen carefully, Tubal" he said, grabbing my gaberdine in both his hands. "We both know that Antonio is a murderer.

We also know that no judgment will ever be passed against him in Venice. Nor is my scheme likely to alter that. For he has three or four argosies on the high seas, any one of which will make good the debt three-fold. But if it should happen that all four are destroyed, then surely we can detect God's hand at work. It will be a sign that I am acting with His blessing, that His hand is guiding mine as I finally extract justice for Zebulum. Ha! With the court's permission! Can you not acknowledge the beauty of it? And, yes, the irony, the blessed irony of it. They will curse me as a blood-thirsty Jew, as I cut out Antonio's heart, little knowing that I am the agent of divine justice. Ho, Tubal, to hell with them all."

What else could I do? I promised him the money.

****

Shylock collected the ducats on Monday. On Tuesday he handed them to Antonio. By Wednesday he was my client.

Also on Tuesday – the night of his departure for Belmont – Bassanio organized a farewell dinner, to which he invited Shylock. Why did he invite Shylock? Perhaps because Shylock's money – actually my money – had enabled the whole enterprise; because he was the key, the sine qua non. But why – in God's name – did Shylock accept the invitation, that is the bigger mystery? Had he not, by his own account, rebuffed a previous invitation with the words, "I will buy with you, sell with you, talk with you, walk with you, and so following: but I will not eat with you, drink with you, nor pray with you"?

"What changed your mind, Shylock?" I said.

He was sitting in the client's chair. There was no sun to offer light – it was after midnight – only a single flame that danced on the head of a candle. But it brought no illumination. As shutters make private the secret life of a room, so Shylock's hands concealed his face, and the emotions that showed upon it.

"Stop torturing me with your questions, Tubal," he said, his voice emerging through the bars of his fingers. "Do you think I have not asked myself the same question a thousand thousand times? Why did I go to the house of that prodigal son of a pig? Why did I not heed my dream that seemed particularly ill-omened? It prompted me to warn Jessica to lock all doors and casements, and not to show herself at any window. But it did not persuade me to stay. My last words to her still ring in my ears, 'Do as I bid you, shut doors after you, fast bind, fast find'."

His hands formed fists and banged upon his forehead.

"But of course when I came home she was nowhere to be found," he said. "I ran through the streets, half hysterical – a man turned mother – but found no help from onlookers, only insolence and mockery. What did Lucan call our children? Hostages given to fortune, or something like. Then it struck me that the invitation to dine with Bassanio was but a ruse to draw me from the house, leaving my daughter – my Jessica – alone and unprotected, easy prey to his minions. And then I remembered what he and Antonio had done to poor Zebulum."

The chair could no longer contain him.

"They will hold her until the day that Antonio's debt comes due," he said, as he staggered to the window. "And if – by some miracle – it should be forfeit, they will offer to sell my daughter back to me for three thousand ducats."

Parting the Venetian blind, he looked down upon the Fondamenta di Cannaregio, and at the oases of light beyond. "She is out there somewhere, Tubal," he said. "Can you find her for me? She's all I have left of Leah. Tubal, you must find my little girl."

"I will do my best," I said. "I will promise you that. But it is no good running from door to door like an unhoused lunatic. There must be method in our madness. Have you informed the authorities of Jessica's disappearance?"

Shylock groaned, and slumped back into the empty chair. Then he laughed. "Think you otherwise?" he said. "Am I not a man of the law? I went straight to the Duke. He looked at me, as if I were a land-rat strayed into his palace, but he did agree to accompany me to the port, where Bassanio's vessel was docked. Too late, too late. It was already under sail. Antonio was still at the quayside, watching it diminish. He swore to the Duke that Jessica was not on board. Then he said – with a smirk, I swear – that my amorous – that's the very word he used, 'amorous', as if my daughter were a common whore – that my amorous daughter had been seen in a gondola with a knave called Lorenzo. But they could not tell me where to find her. Nor why she had not come home. Could it be true, Tubal, that she has abandoned her father, and her faith for a creature like that?"

"God forbid," I said.

Shylock arose again, and – in his misery and despair – hit the wall, not with his fists, but with his head.

"Instead of knocking your brains out," I said, "perhaps you could use them to recall anything out of the ordinary that may have occured yesterday."

"Not a thing, not a thing," said Shylock, "except that my man, Launcelot, left my service to enter that of Bassanio."

"You call that nothing?" I said. "He could have betrayed the secrets of your house to Bassanio's men, and even provided them with a key."

"The man is a clown, Tubal," said Shylock, "who thinks with his stomach. That is why I let Bassanio have him, so that he would eat through his purse, as a horse eats through a nose-bag of hay."

"The fact that he played the clown for you, does not mean that he is a clown for others," I said. "I'll wager he knows something."

Shylock was ready to storm Bassanio's residence at once, but I persuaded him to remain patient until sunrise, at which time the gates of the Ghetto would be unlocked.

We made ourselves known to Bassanio's man, and Launcelot was summoned. He had brains, but no skill in dissembling. When he denied any knowledge of Jessica's disappearance, it was evident to us both that he was lying. With his new master absent on matrimonial business, there was no authority to prevent us from frog-marching him back to the Ghetto.

He was a big man, but he was built of fat, not muscle, and he lacked the strength to resist us. He kept calling upon his father to come to his aid, but his father was either not in earshot, or unwilling to take the risk. The hardest part was persuading him to mount the stairs to my office. I think he feared for his life. Once there we bound him to a chair. As soon as breath returned to his body he begain to wail: "God protect me from the Jews!"

Shylock was in no mood to comfort him.

"If you don't want to die," he said, "tell me what Bassanio and his band of thieves have done with my daughter."

"Your daughter was kind," said Launcelot, "ergo she could not have been yours."

Shylock, in a rage, began to box Launcelot's ears.

"What good will that do?" I said.

Shylock stared at me, the ungutted candle reflected in

both eyes, as if his very soul were aflame within him. "Tubal," he said, "I fear you will never unsheath that dagger you wear so boldly, even when your blood is hot. So give it here. Mine is near boiling."

"Do you hear that Launcelot?" I said. "Shall I do as he demands?"

The fat man began to bawl, as a baby does when it is hungry.

"Spare me, good sirs," he cried, "for all I did was act the go-between. Jessica – I mean your daughter – handed me a letter and a ducat, and bade me give the former to a fine fellow named Lorenzo, who was to dine with you at Bassanio's. Lorenzo, for his part, ordered me to deliver an immediate reply. I was to tell your daughter that he would not fail her. In what I did not know, though it is no secret now."

"So it is true," said Shylock, "my daughter has eloped with a Christian?"

I approached Launcelot.

"Wither did they flee," I said, "if not to Belmont?"

He remained silent. My hand snatched at the hilt of my dagger. It was an involuntary act, which frightened me almost as much as it frightened Launcelot.

"Genoa," he said. "I overheard Lorenzo boast to his cronies that he was taking his new bride there."

I lifted the dagger meaning to sever Launcelot's bonds. But he did not arise, or even thank me, for my gesture had caused him to faint dead away.

"Bride?" said Shylock. "Woe piles upon woe." But he ever was a practical man. "Why Genoa?" he said.

I shook my head.

"You must go there, Tubal," he said, "and redeem my daughter."

I explained that I was not now – nor ever had been – in the redemption business. I was a private eye, pure and simple. I handed Shylock the usual contract.

"It'll cost you two hundred ducats a day plus expenses," I said.

****

My wife packed my bag. My children – bless them – begged for presents. I put on my hat, made of rust-coloured felt, wrapped an orange kerchief around the crown, kissed my wife and my children, then quit the house, the Ghetto, and – within the hour – Venice itself.

How pampered are its citizens, who travel everywhere by gondola. It is true that putrid smells often arise from the canals, but their waters are mostly placid, and a cooling breeze is frequently in evidence. I was soon to discover that the experience of a traveller on land is very different. My chaise was cramped, the road uneven, the air more dust than ether. If the blinds were lowered the heat within grew one degree short of Gehenna, but if they were left raised foul odours – discharged at regular intervals from the rear ends of over-worked and ill-fed horses – found entry.

I recognised my travelling companion as the very merchant who had gleefully broadcast Shylock's public distress, when my friend first discovered that his daughter was missing. He recognised me too, if not by name, then as a Jew, and acted as if the only visible part of me were my hat, which advertised my tribe.

At Verona, the first of countless stages, the horses were replaced; likewise I exchanged my tell-tale hat for a non-descript barrette noire. As soon as our journey resumed,

Solanio – for it was he – suddenly became affable, and began to converse with me as if a different person were now seated beside him. He observed that the digestion of the new horses was no improvement upon that of their predecessors, but took pains to assure me that his suffering – he used the word "suffering" – would be well-rewarded, when he finally presented his merchandise from the Far East before the cities of the West. Every time the vetturino failed to properly navigate a half-buried boulder he winced, not from discomfort, but from fear that his precious Chinese porcelain should come to grief, and with it his expectations. I cursed my bones, but could not find it within myself to wish him ill. He too was travelling all the way to Genoa: the further from Venice, the higher the prices.

After several days of unlooked-for intimacy the chaise crested a summit, and we beheld a sight. The prospect was not serene, as the prospect Venice is serene; but it was superb in a way that Venice is not superb. From our vantage point we beheld an amphitheatre of civilization, a vast city that plunged towards a great bay, into which molos extended like the pincers of crabs. Between these jetties ships rocked at anchor; most single-masted skips, but some three-masted galleons, provisioned for voyages of discovery.

The city itself seemed to consist entirely of palaces and churches. What made the sight so stupendous was the vertiginious quality of the ground upon which the buildings were constructed. They seemed to stand proud in defiance of all known natural laws. It appeared as if the city of Genoa was not the product of architects and engineers, but was dreamed into being by the collective will of its inhabitants. Without their concentrated energy Genoa would be nothing more than rubble and dust.

On a promontory at the far end of the Cape del Faro, the ancient lighthouse pulsed like a heartbeat. The Gulf was a deep ultramarine, upon which wavelets sat like fringes of icing sugar. From our lofty mountain peak all looked beautiful and good, as the world had seemed to God on the first days of creation, but I knew too well that closer inspection would reveal repetition of behaviour that brought down the Great Flood upon humanity. I knew too that somewhere in that tumultuous city was Jessica. Perhaps a captive, more likely a willing convert. What I didn't know was how to find her.

Soon the chill and resinous air of the heights was replaced by more maritime odours, and not long afterwards we spotted white-washed cottages spaced amongst orchards of olive trees. As we descended further we entered a sweet realm of orange groves and villas, and then the gates of the great city itself.

We ran parallel with what can only be described as a palisade of palaces, and then disembarked at our final stage, where porters vied for our business. Solanio had plenty of employment to offer, while I had nothing to carry but a single bag. We took our leave of one another, not without some regret. He proceeded to a well-lit auberge frequented by other merchants, while I made my way down darker alleys.

The inn I happened upon was accessed by a steep flight of ill-made steps. Reaching the top I discovered a trap-door, which opened upon a public room. I entered head and shoulders first, and immediately put an end to all conversation. Eight men were seated at a long table. All stared at me as if I were a demon newly discharged from the underworld. I asked if the proprietor was present, and thereby acquired accommodation. It would have been better for me if I had not, but so much worse for the bedbugs.

After dinner – a crime against the palate – I wandered back to the auberge on the Via Dante where Solanio was bedded, in hopes of catching him afoot. I was not disappointed. He was clearly well-acquainted with the city, and he all but ended my surveillance on two or three occasions, but I managed to stay on his trail until he reached his goal in the Piazza Embriaci.

Once the square had been dominated by a castle decreed by the knight, Guglielmo degli Embriaci, whose siege-engine was supposed to have facilitated the capture of Jerusalem in 1099. But time and neglect had delapidated its mighty walls, and all that now remained of it was the Torre degli Embriaci, at the foot of which was a rectangle of light. Solanio strode boldly into it, like a Christian entering heaven, and I slipped in behind, like his shadow.

As I had always suspected, heaven turned out to be a gambler's paradise. Candles were everywhere, like ghosts with burning hair, their passion multiplied a thousand-fold by well-placed mirrors. In this temple of fortune – both good and ill – dice were rolled, cards dealt, wheels spun, and purses cut. The saved emitted whoops of joy, while the damned groaned as only the damned know how.

Among the latter, arm-in-arm like newly-weds, were Lorenzo and Jessica, he slicked and oiled, she flushed with wine and hot-blood. I slithered through the crowd until I happened upon a dimly-lit niche, from where I could observe Jessica unobserved. Solanio, meanwhile, approached his friends, both of whom embraced him as if he were a hostage new-released from a distant captivity. Solanio must have asked if luck were with them, for both shook their heads vigorously. Then this third party placed his hand on Lorenzo's arm, and drew him slightly aside, perhaps to advise him that a Venetian Jew had been his travelling companion.

At the same time Jessica waged fourscore ducats on a roll of the dice, and was instantly divorced from them all. She turned over her purse, and became desperate when no coins tumbled out. Seeing her behave in so petulant a manner I recalled some remarks of Rabbi Leone Modena, to the effect that there is no better test for human character than the way the gambler reveals himself – or herself – at play. Jessica was also revealing herself in other ways, I could not help but note. Her gown was cut low, after the fashion of gentile courtesans, so that each of her breasts was seen to be in possession of a roughed eye-brow, petulantly arched.

I reckoned the possibilities of wresting her away from Lorenzo and his ally, and considered them remote. Made remoter still by the fact that Jessica showed no inclination to be elsewhere, or any sign that she would welcome my intervention. On the contrary she would probably scream blue murder, whereupon her companions would likely denounce me as a Jew, and I would be hung from the nearest perpendicular by the mob.

Patience seemed to be my only weapon, and I spent the following day trailing Solanio as he disposed of his oriental wares. When night fell he returned – as anticipated – to the Torre degli Embriaci, a far richer man than he had been when he arose. Lorenzo was awaiting him there, but of Jessica there was no sign. It was apparent that Lorenzo was also richer than he had appeared yesterday, or had recently become one of fortune's darlings. But where was Shylock's darling? Her absence was beginning to alarm me, and I comforted myself with the supposition that she had renounced gambling, or feeling unwell, had taken to her bed.

At the close of proceedings I chose to follow Lorenzo to his lodgings on the ill-named Via San Lorenzo; an undertaking hampered by clouds that obscured the stars, rain that curtained the streets, and ground that had grown treacherous underfoot. I offered the proprietor of the establishment – a man who seemed built out of blubbery quoits – a respectable bribe, and learned in return that the pair had left in the morning, but that only one – the signor – had returned in the afternoon. This was not good news.

In my frustration I decided to return to Solanio's auberge, and do what I did not yet know. With each step I took, I cursed the very notion of patience. Why had I not acted last night, when I had Jessica within my grasp? I swore at prudence. I poured scorn upon my cowardice. Infuriated and blinded by self-loathing, I over-stepped the auberge, even though it was advertised with crucibles of fire, and found myself at the very end of the Via Dante, outside an ivy-clad house, dimly lit, and far from palatial.

****

I thought myself well-cloaked by the darkness, but someone with a practised eye picked out a solid shape amid the insubstantial night. Without introduction he began a minor oration: "You do well to pause and wonder, signor, for in that modest abode once lived our state's greatest son, and the world's most daring navigator. You know his name already, but I shall pronounce it anyway, for the very sound of it – like soft winds hissing in the sails – gives me ease: Christopher Columbus."

From which I quickly deduced that the speaker was a mariner without a berth, a seaman gone to seed.

"Ah, signor," he continued, "if only Genoa had been willing to supply him with the ships and men he so earnestly requested, then the New World would have belonged to us, not Spain, and all the riches thereof. And you and I, signor, you and I would have been princes, a Pizzaro or a Cortez. Instead of broken men who wander the city dreaming of voyages that never were."

Obviously he thought that I too was a vagabond. But before I had the opportunity to disabuse him I was distracted by a great internal illumination. Of a sudden I was privy to it all; to the plot against Jessica, and her present whereabouts (more or less). Without even acknowledging the garrulous stranger – who had unconsciously unlocked the mystery – I turned my back upon him, and began to run as fast as I dared in the direction of the Molo Vecchio.

My thoughts were these: as Venice traded with China, so did Genoa with the Americas. Among the products it dealt in were slaves; black slaves for the mines, and white slaves for the men. Is it any wonder that I ran?

But just as abruptly I stopped. What did I know of ships, who had never been on anything larger than a gondola? I hurridly retraced my steps up the steeply ranked cobbles, and reached the Via Dante breathless, where – thank God – the old salt was still cataloguing the many luxuries that had eluded him.

"Signor," I said, "I bring you an offer with no promise of reward. A lady has fallen prey to wicked men, and her life is at stake. Are you willing to help me mount a rescue? Do you have the stomach for one more bold adventure?"

"Thundering typhoons!" he bellowed like old Boreas himself. "You have breathed life back into my deflated spirit. If there are wenches to be saved, I'm your man."

He was not fleet-footed, but he knew the path. Our passage was further assisted by the moon, new-burnished by clouds that streamed across its face like sheets of shammy-leather. It also made visible four full-rigged ships anchored in ragged formation around a man-o'-war.

"She'll be on one of those, for sure," said the old salt. "The man-o'-war gives it away. The last flotilla that approached the Americas with a cargo of women was boarded by pirates, and every last one of those unfortunates was raped fore and aft. No respect was shown to virgins either. By the time the ships made land the merchandise had lost the best part of its value. To prevent a repetition of that tragedy the owners have commissioned a guardian angel."

"How will I know which one of the four hides Jessica?" I said.

"I have the nose," he said, "and as I now can observe, you have the purse."

Even from where we stood we could see there was much activity on the molo; torches by the dozen were dancing through the darkness like so many drunken fireflies.

"Signor," said the former sailor. "The wind has changed course, since the rain ceased. It is now set fair. Look how fore and main sails are being unfurled. After that the halyards and the braces will be belayed. Finally anchors will be weighed and catted. And then this lady of yours will be lost to you forever."

At the entrance to the molo my companion spotted an old soak, perched upon a milestone.

"Half-a-dozen voyages I made with him as my first mate," said the ex-seaman. "He'll have the answer. For a price."

Which I gladly paid on Shylock's behalf.

Seeing his former commander's approach, the man

removed the clay pipestem from his mouth, arose, spread his arms, and exclaimed: "Captain Merluzzo, is it really you?"

The two old companions hugged for several moments, after which words were exchanged, money deposited, and a name given.

"She's on the Santa Lucia," said the man I now knew to be Captain Merluzzo.

The Santa Lucia was, of course, the furthest ship on the molo. Her name was chiseled on her stern, under the captain's mullioned windows, and again on the bow beneath a bare-breasted figure-head. Captain Merluzzo figured the vessel's weight to be in the region of two hundred tons. A fo'c'sle and a poop towered above her main deck. Between them were three masts, whose sails were already lapping the briny air. Frayed ropes creaked with the strain of keeping them land-locked. The night smelled of things to come.

"The gangplank has not yet been raised," noted Captain Merluzzo. "Also in our favour is the fact that the crew is preoccupied with making final preparations for the long voyage. Once on board we must proceed with confidence, as if we were their ship-mates."

The noise on the main deck was an orchestra of discord, what with the waves, the wind, the whip-crack of sails, and the crew chorusing shanties. Enough, you would have thought, to drown the sound of Captain Merluzzo splintering the door to the companionway with a carpenter's maul, carelessly left nearby. But, alas, the hammering alerted an idle sailmaker, who quickly realized our intention.

For the first time in my life I drew my dagger, and pointed it menacingly at another human being. He stepped back, not in fear, but only to better unscabbard his cutlass. He thrust at me without discipline, obviously uncertain whether he favoured disembowelment or beheading. His second swing came closer to my neck. Who knows? His third attempt might well have succeeded in separating my head from my shoulders, and sending the orphaned comet on a bloody orbit across the deck, if Captain Merluzzo had not laid him out with a blow behind the ear.

Now the way was clear to midships where – we had been told – seventy girls were hammocked. I tumbled down the ladder, raised myself to my full height, and walloped my own scalp on a cross-beam. Regaining my senses I saw that I had fallen into something like a chapelle ardente. Whereas most were high-vaulted, this was low-ceilinged. What light there was came from guttering candles. Instead of a Doge or other great personage lying in state, there appeared a bivouac of overweight chrysalids suspended in mid-air.

I threw a name into that obscurity: "Jessica!"

And out of the obscurity came the reply: "Thank God, Tubal. Did Lorenzo send you?"

A head emerged from one of the cacoons, then another, and a third. The braver materialized fully and placed their feet upon the rough timbers. Splinters entered their soles, and drew blood; a presage in miniature of what would befall them if they did not seize the opportunity lately provided of flight.

Instead they screamed. The man who finds a gentle way to end female hysteria will quickly rival Croesus. I am not that man.

"Quiet, ladies," I pleaded. "We have come as rescuers, not ravishers."

They did not credit my words, and screamed all the more. Some of these banshees were clothed in white smocks, others in fleshings, or – in some extreme cases – the very flesh itself.

But when they saw Jessica unharmed in my arms, and of her own volition, they calmed sufficiently for us to usher them up the steps to freedom. Captain Merluzzo led the party. I followed the naked buttocks of the last.

Surveying his small kingdom from the poop deck, the captain of the Santa Lucia spotted the departure of his raison d'être, and ordered his crew to stop it. Those who heard his command above the general commotion, took position between our troop and the gangplank. They numbered twenty or more, and were armed to the teeth.

Captain Merluzzo shook my hand. "You have given me new life," he said, "but even if it ends on the night it began, I shall die a happy man."

I advised Jessica to jump overboard when I met my end.

My bold companion raised his maul, and prepared to sell his life dearly. I unsheathed my dagger for the second time, and recited the Shema: "Hear, O Israel, the Lord is God, the Lord is One".

But as it turned out, we did not lead the charge. The advance guard came from the ranks. As Jessica later explained, not all the women were virgins, and not all were prisoners. Some were already prostitutes. Others were ready to whore themselves in exchange for passage to the New World. They actually wanted to sail with the Santa Lucia, but – God bless them – were prepared to sacrifice themselves in order to assure the escape of those who did not. They flung themselves upon our astonished antagonists, who – forgetting themselves – first dropped their weapons and then their breeches.

Once he had assured himself that my path was clear,

Captain Merluzzo elected to change sides, and commenced mortal combat with one of the ungirdled Amazons, who employed whorish tactics to first inflame and then subdue.

"I never thought to see such a night as this again," he gasped as we parted. "Tell me, did God send you?"

"No," I said, "only Shylock."

A simple fact that Jessica refused to believe. Counting her twenty women were restored to terra sancta that night, but I only had an interest in one of them.

My immediate concern was to escort her to my inn. The sky was now clear but the air was chill, and Jessica stood shivering in her shift. She was barefoot too. Although she sometimes called me Uncle Tubal, it was my father who was Shylock's contemporary, not me. I was her senior, to be sure, but only by a dozen years, and was certainly not insensible to the attributes that would have made her such a valuable commodity in the bordellos of New Spain.

To carry her would not have been beyond my strength, but would have taxed other powers best monopolized by my wife. So I gave her my cloak, and told her to mind where she stepped.

We discussed the night's excitements, and spoke of the great battle we had won. I told her the news from the Rialto.

Back in my chamber the spiders had woven a welcome mat. But Jessica only wanted to know why her beau had not busied himself in some like manner.

"Where is Lorenzo?" she said. "Why is he not here?"

"Because he has no idea that you are," I said.

"But he comissioned you and the brave captain with my rescue, did he not?" she said.

"He did not," I said. "Shylock did."

Jessica shook her head.

"But Lorenzo said that my father had disowned me," she said, "and shown the world that I was dead to him by sitting shiva – of course he did not use that word."

"Then he lied," I said. "Your father is angry, but he is also broken-hearted. He badly wants you back."

"But he cannot have me," said Jessica. "I belong to another."

The room was not furnished with chairs, or any other comforts, so I motioned for her to sit on my pallet, thereby awakening a whole continent of verminous life.

"Are you Lorenzo's wife?" I said.

"In the eyes of God," she said.

"What does that mean?" I said.

"He has known me," she said.

"Like Adam knew Eve?" I said.

She hesitated.

"It would be better to say, 'I knew him'," she said. "To save him from committing the sin of Onan, I swallowed his seed."

Dear God, I thought, already he has begun instructing her in the arts required to please those who will be paying for their pleasure. But I was curious to know how he had guiled her into such a pastime.

"Lorenzo persuaded me that it would be preferable for us to commence new lives in the New World," she said, "since we were both orphans, and had no ties in the Old. He secured our passage on the Santa Lucia, and explained that he had best reserve his full marital rights for the other side, lest I fall pregnant. Seasickness, he said, was curse enough."

I could forebear no longer.

"Foolish girl!" I said. "There is but a single reason Lorenzo did not split your hymen, and it is not the one he gave. You were spared because virginity is valued higher than rubies in the stews of the Americas. Do you not understand, Jessica? Lorenzo sold you into white slavery."

She rose from the infested cot and began to beat me with her little fists.

"Lies," she cries, "lies, lies, lies!"

"Now I know why they say the truth hurts," I said, as another blow landed on my nose, "but nothing you do will change the fact that Lorenzo was in the Torre degli Embriaci gambling away his new-found wealth, while you were a prisoner on the Santa Lucia."

"More lies!" she cried, but her protestations were beginning to lack conviction.

"Think, Jessica," I said, "can you explain why Lorenzo was not counted among your redeemers?"

She laughed, as if my question were the question of a simpleton.

"His face was known to the crew," she said, "and would have betrayed your intentions."

"But he knew nothing of our intentions," I said. "Why would he when his were the opposite?"

"At last I truly believe that my father sent you, Tubal," she said, "to poison my mind against Lorenzo."

I blew out the candles, but neither of us could sleep. Jessica stretched restlessly on my mattress, waiting only for the morn, when she could return to the arms of the very man who had betrayed her. While I lay open-eyed upon the floor, rehearsing arguments designed to prevent this act of amorous folly. Then there was the question of retrieving the glittering dowry Jessica had so carelessly – and illegally – bestowed upon her worthless paramour. Above all, how was I to convince a love-struck girl to abandon the object of her desire, and accompany me back to Venice, and her father's house? In the topsy-turvy world she now inhabited, her enslaver had become her liberator, and her protector her jailer.

Neither of us spoke. The only sounds were of our irregular breathing, and of rodents scratching their way from wall to wall.

When the sun rose I knew she could be restrained no longer. Arising also, I elected to escort her back to Lorenzo myself, in the hope that his discomfort would become apparent even to her, and act as antidote to the venom he had already poured into her ear.

"See how Apollo still blushes," said Jessica, "for all the sins committed while his back was turned."

Her mood had lightened as soon as we stepped out into the street; it was as though anticipation had usurped reality, and she was already in the arms of her lover.

"Come, Uncle Tubal," she said, placing hers through mine, "we must not keep Lorenzo waiting. Let us hurry and catch him at his toilet. I cannot wait to see the joyful expression when he realizes that I am safe, and restored to him."

Fool that I was, I felt guilty, even cruel, for the method I was employing to crush her trusting nature, to make a laughing-stock of her idealism. I foresaw her despair, and the comfort I would offer, and the opportunity I would take to spirit her away.

Walking briskly we turned on to the Via San Lorenzo, which was already as over-crowded as hell's inner circle. A few of our fellow pedestrians took cognisance of Jessica's outlandish appearance – her shift was concealed by one of my lighter cloaks, and her feet by a pair of my black boots – but most let her pass unremarked. Even the proprietor of the inn where her seducer lodged barely gave the silly girl a second glance. He was the same fellow I had bribed but yesterday, and he afforded me a sly smile.

Jessica bounded up the stairs, and without troubling to knock, opened the door to her erstwhile room. My best hope was that Lorenzo would be abed with a local trollop. Failing that I hoped to discover him packing his bags in preparation for flight. What I had not expected was to see him on bent knees apparently at his orisons.

Turning to face Jessica, he said unblushingly: “Have my prayers been answered? Is it really you?”

In desperation I attempted to ground Jessica as she took flight in his direction.

Encircling her possessively, he began to shout: “A Jew! A Jew! A dog Jew has come to murder my wife; to end her life for deciding to abandon the wicked faith of deicides.”

Downstairs I heard the sweaty proprietor haul himself from his chair, and summon armed men.

“Oh Jessica,” I said, “such a mistake you are making.”

“Not as big as the one you will be making if you do not leave now,” said Lorenzo.

The last thing I saw as I backed into the Via San Lorenzo – my dagger once more pointed at my enemies – was Jessica’s head framed in the casement above, and the last thing that I heard as I raced along it, was the sound of her laughter.

****

And the last person I wanted to encounter when I returned to Venice was her father. Needless to say, he was the first. And he saw me before I saw him.

“How now Tubal!” he said, “what news from Genoa? Hast thou found my daughter?”

I could not bring myself to tell him the bare fact that I had arrested his daughter, only to lose her again. God help me, I lied: "I often came where I did hear of her, but could not find her."

"No news of her? Why so!" he cried. "And I know not what's spent in the search: why thou – loss upon loss! The thief gone with so much, and so much to find the thief, and no satisfaction, no revenge, nor no ill luck stirring but what lights o' my shoulders, no sighs but my way o' breathing, no tears but o' my shedding."

Although my untruth had occasioned this outburst, I felt absolved by Shylock's anger. How dare he question the cost of my investigation? Had he forgotten so quickly that the Tubals had financed his loan to Antonio? I decided to pay him back in kind.

I said: "Your daughter spent in Genoa, as I heard, one night, fourscore ducats."

"Thou stick'st a dagger in me," said Shylock, clutching at his chest, "fourscore ducats at a sitting, fourscore ducats."

Nor was that the conclusion of my revenge. I told Shylock that I had returned to Venice in the company of one of Antonio's creditors.

"He showed me a ring," I said, "that he had of your daughter for a monkey."

"Out upon her! – thou torturest me Tubal," cried Shylock. "It was my turquoise, I had it of Leah when I was a bachelor: I would not have given it for a wilderness of monkeys."

The sight of his misery undilute caused me to repent of my indignation, and I reminded Shylock that other men had ill luck too. I told him that I had also heard in Genoa that one of Antonio's argosies had come to grief, and that the same creditor who had shown me Leah's ring, had assured me that Antonio was certainly undone.

"I thank thee good Tubal," said Shylock, "good news, good news: ha ha! heard in Genoa! I will have the heart of him if he forfeit, and Zebulum will have his revenge."

****

And his plan might even have succeeded if Bassanio's new wife hadn't entered the court at the last minute, in the guise of Balthazar, a lawyer's apprentice. At first, with honeyed rhetoric, she prosletysed the cause of mercy, but Shylock rebuffed her pleas, insisting upon justice; justice for him, and – all unspoken – for Zebulum too. Counterfeiting surrender Balthazar – rather Portia – counseled Antonio to lay bare his bosom. Would Shylock really have plunged the blade through flesh to beating heart? To this day, I do not know the answer. But I suspect – judging from my own experience – that he was by then a passenger of the drama, and would not have been able to stay his hand, even if that had been his dearest wish.

In any event, Shylock never got the chance to strike, for just then Portia introduced a conceit, the like of which I had not heard since I stood with Rabbi Leone Modena on the Calle Vallaresso: "Take then thy bond, take thou thy pound of flesh, but in the cutting it, if thou dost shed one drop of Christian blood, thy lands and goods are confiscate."

This pronouncement was the end of Shylock, and his vision of justice. Now it was Portia's turn to demand it, all thought of mercy gone; for the Jew there was to be no hint of mercy, no gentle dew, merely justice. In the end the court stripped Shylock of everything, even his Jewishness. How he passed empty days as one of the new baptized I do not know, but on the sabbath I often saw him standing outside the synagogue, silently mouthing the prayers that were being declaimed within.

And what of his daughter, what of the girl I had failed to restore unto him? Even though Jessica was known to have returned to Venice, she made no effort to contact Shylock. There were even reports that she had been seen with Lorenzo at Belmont, home to the woman who had destroyed her father, and to the man who had robbed Zebulum of threescore years.

Like Zebulum, Jessica tugged at my conscience, caused me to lay abed but awake, reliving my defeat, and seeking strategies that – if pursued – would have altered the course of events. Insomnia was bad enough, but sleep was worse, for with sleep came dreams, out-of-control dreams that had me do things I repented upon awakening.

****

Then one fine day Jessica flounced into my office. Seeing her in the alternate light and shade created by the Venetian blind, put me in mind of that graceful but strange creature, the zebra. But as she drew nearer I noted that she was in fact dishevelled, and that her composure was a fragile thing.

“Oh, Tubal,” she said, and dissolved into tears.

I jumped from my seat and clasped her to me, thinking to offer her comfort, and in so doing felt at last the body I had deemed too tempting in Genoa. My embrace had been temporary in intent, but it seemed she did not want to let me go.

“Uncle Tubal,” she said, so that I could feel her moist breath buttering my cheek, and fogging my brain, “I owe you an apology. You were right about Lorenzo. As was my father when he said: ‘I have a daughter – would any of the stock of Barrabas had been her husband rather than a Christian’. But I took no heed of either of you, and now I am the wife of one.”

"Apology accepted," I said, managing at last to untangle myself. "Is there anything else I can do for you?"

"You remember that paper Antonio forced my father to sign?" she said, walking back and forth, like a captive beast in a cage. "The one that made over all he possessed to the 'gentleman who lately stole his daughter', and to the ingratiate herself, in the event of his death? When he signed that document, Tubal, he signed his own death warrant. You think that maybe I am exaggerating? That this is all the imagining of a troubled conscience? Well listen, Tubal, listen well."

So saying she sat at last, and delivered an episode from life at Belmont.

"Last night," she said, "as they arose from the dinner table, Lorenzo began to speak about my father with Antonio and Bassanio. Knowing their destination I excused myself, hurried along a torch-lit corridor, passing tapestries that depicted scenes of hunting and battle. Reaching the library I concealed myself behind an arras. The three merchants followed, and seated themselves close to the log fire. The flames cast grotesque shadows, making them look as hellish as their thoughts. For it was in that spot, surrounded by books of law, that I over-heard their plot to hasten my father's end.

"After they had toasted the success of the enterprise, Bassanio inquired of Lorenzo why he had married a Jewess.

"'For the same reason you wed Portia,' he said; 'to become heir to her father's wealth.' With those words all the dreams – all the hopes – of my youth were turned to ash. If Lorenzo married me with a cold heart, what else might that cold heart have him do? Do you think he will rest when he has killed my father, Tubal, or think you that am I in danger too?"

“I think you are in danger too,” I said, “but first things first. I must start to watch over your father. And you must become a spy in your own house, listening until you know for certain the very time and place of the sticking point.”

She hugged me again before we parted.

“You are a good man, Tubal,” she said.

The following week she sent me a note, via Launcelot, who had returned to her employ.

“The conspirators have found that tomorrow Shylock will be visiting an establishment on the Calle Vallaresso,” it read. “Lorenzo has elected to strike the fatal blow as the clock chimes midnight.”

****

And it came to pass at midnight, just as Jessica had predicted. From my vantage point in the shadows I observed Lorenzo as he began to overhaul a stooped figure in a black cloak. I kept thinking of the last words Shylock had uttered in court: “I pray you give me leave to go from hence, I am not well.” That was how he looked now, not well. I called upon Lorenzo to stop, which he did. Only to turn with his stiletto already to hand. I unsheathed my own dagger, and closed upon him. He thrust, I side-stepped, and without forethought lunged at him. The blade struck him between the ribs, and did not cease until it had stopped his heart. I shall not easily forget the look of astonishment upon his face, as his corpse slipped through my arms to the ground.

Ahead of me Shylock was on his knees, but when he turned to thank me, I beheld neither beard nor wrinkles, but skin as white as a lily; for the face beneath the hood belonged not to him, but to his daughter. Realizing then the truth of the matter, I began to shake. I was no saviour, but an assassin.

"Why do you look so horrified, Tubal," she said, "when you have just saved my life?"

My mind – all unbidden – began to test horrid conjectures: what if she had stitched together her story, what if it were as mythical as a scene on one of Belmont's tapestries, what if Jessica not Lorenzo had been the only begetter of Lorenzo's plot?

"You have not been honest with me, Jessica," I said, "so how can I be confident that Lorenzo really said what you said he said."

"Was the blade in his hand not proof enough?" she said.

"It is equally possible that he took the man who challenged him to be a murderer – correctly as it turned out – and looked only to defend himself," I said.

"You may call yourself whatever comforts you," she said, "but as far as I am concerned, you are my champion. I doubted you once, Tubal, as you doubt me presently. But now I am sure."

She arose from her kneeling position, and embraced me.

"No," I said, but she persisted.

"How you are shaking, Tubal," she said, "like a man in need of succour."

"Not from you," I said.

"Do not be so obstinate, Tubal," she said, "unless you want the authorities to find you here. What do you think they will make of a Jew standing over the body of a Christian?"

"Much the same as I do," I said.

Nevertheless, I allowed her to lead me down deserted alleys, all the way back to my office. I unlocked the door and saw – or rather didn't see – that only black light slid through the Venetian blinds.

"Tubal," said Jessica, "where are the candles?"

When a few were lit she noticed, for the first time, that the left sleeve of my doublet was heavy with blood.

"Why, Tubal," she said, "you are hurt."

It was a matter of indifference to me, but I did not stop her from removing my jacket and the blouse beneath. The blood was still wet, but no longer flowing freely. The wound itself was in the upper arm, where an observant Jew winds his phylacteries every morning.

"This was a thrust meant for your heart," said Jessica.

It occured to me that I was now standing just as Antonio had stood before the Duke, awaiting judgment, his life seemingly in the balance. In which case my Portia was Jessica, and the portion at stake – or so it felt to me – was not my life, but my very soul. And I feared that I was an irresolute guardian.

"You must think me a poor nurse," said Jessica, whose own hands were as bloodied as my arm, and whose bodice had become as stained as my doublet.

"I am as indifferent to your skills, as I am to my injury," I said.

"In which case I must act for the pair of us," said Jessica, making a bundle of my clothes.

Then she began to remove her own.

"Why do you stare so, Tubal?" she asked. "Have you never seen a woman's breasts before?"

They were perfect in every detail, and drew me to them as if I were a suckling babe, but they were unclean, dyed crimson by my own blood. With an effort I stepped back. Sensing the cause, Jessica laughed.

"Ho, Tubal," she said, "you act as though you had seen the devil in person. Permit me to demonstrate that you are in error."

She snatched my right hand and placed it on the hidden under-carriage of her left breast.

"Do you feel scales, Tubal?" she said.

I do not know what I felt, any more than a dog knows what it feels when it mounts a bitch. All I know is that it was not my seed she sucked into her womb, when we copulated upon the floor, but my will, and – yes – perhaps my soul with it. Did I reason with myself, did I argue thus: 'Tubal, you have already committed murder this night, so why not add adultery to your bill?' I cannot say.

"Are you married, Tubal," said Jessica, when I was still lying all spent atop her.

"I have a wife," I said.

"And I always imagined you a bachelor," she said. "My father never spoke of her."

"I would prefer if you did not speak of her either," I said.

"I understand," she said. "I too have cause for guilt. After all it is not very becoming for a woman, newly widowed, to consort with the very man who put her in that state. If I wished to absolve myself I could call you 'rapist'."

She paused to make an observation.

"Poor Tubal," she said, "you have begun to shake all over again."

"What do you want of me?" I said.

"Foolish man," she said, kissing me. "I already have what I wanted."

"You mean Lorenzo dead?" I said.

"That too," she said. "Was it not you, Tubal, who first tried to convince me of his treachery, and his greed? When I finally accepted that you were right, I resolved that he would never live to enjoy my fortune. I am not a second Portia, Tubal. I would never willingly have called him my lord and my master, and ceded to him all the treasure that my industrious father had accumulated. Maybe your suspicions are correct, and he never uttered the words I put in his mouth, but do you seriously believe that he never thought them? And – knowing what you know – do you think he would not have wished me dead too? Think what you will, Tubal, but to my mind you saved my life tonight."

Perhaps the desire for her was in me from the beginning, but once ignited it knew no bounds. I had supped at Jessica's breasts, and tasted not mother's milk, but my own blood. The evidence was on my lips, which were now painted like a whore's. All restraint was gone. My heart and my kidneys were speckled.

We wrestled all night upon the floor like Jacob and the Angel – except that I was no patriarch, and she no angel – and were still contesting the space when I felt light from the new day lashing my back. No, I was no Jacob. I was not even an Esau. Esau was hairy, but I was hairier still. As I disengaged from Jessica's privates for the last time, I recognised that I was cousin to the monkey that had been had for a ring. It was true! I was no better than a beast, my commandments reduced to a couple: to gratify my appetites, and to survive.

"They will have found your husband's body by now," I said, "and you must be at home when the news comes."

Like it or not, I had become a co-conspirator.

"You know that we have completed but half the job," said Jessica. "The ducats and the jewels are still in my father's possession."

"Where they belong," I said.

But I realized, even as I spoke, that never again would my soul know rest, that the remainder of my life would be plagued by remorse for what I had already done, and what I was yet to do.

"Is it not true that my father would rather have them than a living child?" she said. "Is it not true that he said to you: 'I would my daughter were dead at my foot, and the jewels in her ear, would she were hears'd at my foot, and the ducats in her coffin'? Or were his words misrepresented?"

"Those words were wicked," I said, "but they were words spoken in anger."

"Every breath he draws is drawn in anger," she said. "He knows no other emotion. Sooner or later I am bound to feel the full force of it. Unless . . ."

I knew what was coming next, and no longer had the strength or the will to stop it.

"Tubal," said Jessica, "you must kill my father. Shylock must die."

Tears of the Giraffe

IF A LION COULD speak, wrote the philosopher, we probably could not understand him. Even more so in the case of a giraffe, which is ten feet tall and talks in whispers. But tears are a universal tongue. And young Arnie Oberg understood them well enough, as he witnessed two-year old Markus being snatched from a pair of reticulated giraffes one afternoon in Stockholm Zoo, and dispatched with a single shotgun blast to the head. Giraffes have large eyes, and the tears that fell from those of his parents made mighty splashes. In their inarticulate agony the other reticulates banged their heads against the back wall of their enclosure.

Arnie watched the assassination at the invitation of his older brother. Though only seventeen Stig Oberg was a founder member of the Swedish Nazi Party. Up to that moment Arnie had himself been an unquestioning member of the Hitler Youth. You could even go so far as to say he worshipped the Fuhrer, in a way that he did not worship his father. He had yet to hear the latter call him a member of the Master Race. Unlike Stig, Arnie had no interest in the economic theories of National Socialism, which he found confusing. On the one hand, he was told, Jews controlled the banks, and, through them, the world; on the other they were all Bolsheviks, dedicated to the violent overthrow of capitalism. He began to think you could recognize a Jew by the fact that he had two heads.

No, what appealed to him about National Socialism was its atavism, its wild romance. He loved wandering through the woods surrounding Uppsala, where the Obergs lived, ever hopeful of bumping into a lone wisent or even a pack of wolves. And so was captivated by stories coming out of Berlin Zoo, of the efforts of Lutz Heck and his brother, Heinz, to recreate the auroch, a large horned ox, extinct since 1627. Their method was to back-breed, to excise centuries of domestication from docile oxen, and release the wild beast within. What boy would not wish the same for himself? The eventual aim of the Heck brothers was to reproduce the very creatures painted on the walls of caves by prehistoric man. Arnie saw nothing sinister in this drive to reestablish the purity of the landscape, and of the animals that wandered free within it.

At least until that afternoon in Stockholm Zoo, which did not end with the shooting of Markus. Towards evening a disciple of Lutz Heck arrived from Berlin Zoo to conduct a public autopsy. Knowing of his brother's admiration for Heck's work, Stig had acquired two tickets, one for each of them, by way of a treat. They sat on bales of hay as the anatomist covered his outer garments – some sort of blazer, jodhpurs, and riding boots – with a white apron. Even so he still seemed to gleam from head to toe, like the brass and steel scalpel he was holding. He spoke as he cut, first of all severing the young giraffe's head from its neck, as if it were being punished for some unspeakable crime. Unfortunately the anatomist explained his work in his native tongue, which Stig endeavoured to translate for the benefit of his brother.

"Some of you may think this cruel," he began, "but it is necessary to ensure a healthy population. Eugenics requires a variety of perfect specimens. Otherwise the consequences of in-breeding become apparent. You only have to look at the Jews."

By now the hard-working anatomist was in the process of extracting the giraffe's heart, which he raised up like some Aztec priest.

"As you can imagine," he said, "it has to be extra-large to pump the blood up the giraffe's long neck to its brain. We in Germany are fortunate to have such a one."

Afterwards Arnie learned what happens to those deemed surplus to requirements: their remains are fed to the tigers. But what is the life of a giraffe, alas, when armies clash by night? All Hitler had to do was to invade Poland for Arnie to erase all memory of Markus. With Stig as his guide he followed the progress of the Wehrmacht as it fought its way towards Warsaw. In his wild imaginings he pictured latter-day Vikings subduing hoards of subhuman Slavs. How he rejoiced when Warsaw fell!

The invasion of Denmark, a few months later, was harder to understand, until Stig explained that it was not an act of aggression, but one of fraternal love, designed to protect the population from Churchill and other traitors to the race. The Danes must have grasped this instinctively, he added; how else to account for the fact that they capitulated after only six hours? For some reason it took the Norwegians sixty days and more to fully appreciate Hitler's charitable intentions. Sweden remained officially neutral, of course, but to advertise his allegiance Stig saved the wages from his first job, and purchased a Volkswagen, one as black as the Arctic night.

About that time the memory of Markus flickered briefly to life when Arnie read somewhere that Lutz Heck had been seconded to the zoo in Poland's capital to oversee the transport of those animals he considered of use to Germany. As for the unwanted lions and other innocents? A hunting party was arranged, the cages unlocked, freedom briefly tasted, and just as quickly ended by gun-toting trophy collectors. Arnie knew it to be sacrilegious, but even so he couldn't help hoping that a few of the bears escaped the slaughter. But in truth there was just too much going on elsewhere for the old doubts to linger; World Wars are busy times.

****

Soon after the securing of Norway, when the days were still long, Stig announced that, as a leader of Sweden's Nazi Party, he had been invited to attend an exclusive performance of Hamlet at Helsingor, and proposed taking the whole family with him as a special treat. And so it was. Early one morning they all squeezed into his VW: Arnie in the back alongside his mother; his father in front with the maps. By the time they reached Jonkoping at the southern tip of Lake Vattern – after nearly five hours on the road in a cramped automobile – family solidarity had been replaced by political bickering.

Unlike her sons Mrs Oberg was no fan of Hitler's ideas on racial purity, for the very good reason that her own mother was Jewish. Moreover, she had maternal cousins living in occupied Denmark. She now bitterly regretted keeping the boys' ancestry from them, as if it were a family secret of which to be ashamed. All the more so when they commenced a lusty rendition of that loathsome marching tune, the Horst Wessel Song:

"For the last time, the call to arms is sounded!/ For the fight, we all stand prepared!/ Already Hitler's banners fly over all streets./ The time of bondage will last but a little while now!"

As she listened she began to fear – perhaps for the first time – that her sons' dalliance with Nazism was beginning to harden from a juvenile obsession into an indelible character trait. Were that to happen it would surely break her heart. Mr Oberg also found the Nazi ideology repugnant, and, sensing his wife's disquiet, felt the necessity to say something, to offer guidance beyond that found on maps.

"For God's sake," he said to the boys, "shut up."

They continued to sing regardless, as if consumed by revolutionary zeal.

"Tell me," said Mr Oberg, "what would you do if Hitler were to violate Sweden's neutrality?"

"Nazism like communism is a universal credo," said Stig. "It recognizes no national boundaries or borders. So there is no inherent contradiction between being a Swede and a Nazi."

My boy is no fool, thought Mr Oberg.

"Do you know what the Nazis do to those who oppose them?" said Mrs Oberg. "Not to mention those they deem to be inferiors."

"Arnie is a schoolboy, as was I until a year ago," said Stig. "We are already all too familiar with the smack of firm governance."

And so it went, all through lunch, and all the way down to Helsingborg, where they found two rooms in an old-fashioned hotel, and Mrs Olberg wept in hers.

Next morning they left the car in the harbour and took the ferry to Helsingor, home of the castle Shakespeare called Elsinore (still Kronborg for the Danes). Either way town and castle were overrun by the Wehrmacht. Notwithstanding the fact that they were in uniform they presented themselves as an eager band of young tourists, rather than the invaders that they were. Each time Stig and Arnie passed a group they delighted – much to their parents' displeasure – in greeting it with the Nazi salute and a rousing bark of, "Heil Hitler!" Stig, in acknowledgement of his position within the Swedish Nazi party, was wearing a brown shirt, while Arnie had insisted upon the outfit of the Hitler Youth: black shorts, tan shirt, and a dark kerchief secured with a woggle. So naturally the greeting was returned.

Towards evening they took their seats in the castle's courtyard. The sky was clear and the sun, reddening in the west, caused the massed hair of the soldiers to shine like a field of unharvested wheat. That harvest would come later, and in the east. But for tonight death was confined to the stage. The ghost of Hamlet's father made a spectacular tour of the battlements, pursued by his distraught son. Needless to say, the production was in German, and as at Stockholm Zoo, Stig did his best to keep Arnie abreast of the action.

"The ghost is demanding revenge upon the usurper who murdered him and seduced Hamlet's mother," he whispered.

A request that seemed more than justified when the vile culprit finally showed himself in the next scene: there he was, wearing the dead king's crown, and pawing his former queen. And that was not the worst of it; he also had lank greasy hair, and a nose that could cut a path through the north-west passage. The audience needed no further clues as to what Hamlet meant when he said, "Something is rotten in the state of Denmark". And so, after the play-within-the-play, when Claudius more or less confessed, and Hamlet had his best chance of revenging his father, the audience cried out, as if prompted, "Kill the Jew!" It hurt Mrs Oberg beyond measure to see her sons join in, though Arnie she could forgive, ascribing his bloodthirstiness to youthful ignorance and bad influences. Above all, she blamed herself. There was a collective sigh of relief as Hamlet at last plunged his poison blade into Claudius in Act 5, even though it cost him his own life. And when Fortinbras finally entered to take control of events and the kingdom, dressed as an officer in the Werhmacht, the entire audience – give or take a handful of civilians – followed him across the stage, just as they had done in reality.

****

That handful of civilians grew over the next couple of years, until it merited the name of resistance. Strikes, sabotage and bombings eventually reached such a level that Hitler took notice and said, "No more Mr Nice Guy". Among the many things endangered thereafter were Denmark's democracy, and its Jews. Indeed, a date was set for their mass deportation; October 1 1943. A few days before word was leaked to the attaché for maritime affairs at the German Embassy, the perfectly named GF Duckwitz. No fan of Hitler and his methods, he secretly warned the Jewish community of the fate that awaited. By chance Rosh Hashanah, the Jewish New Year, was approaching, when even secular Jews attended synagogue in hopes of persuading the Almighty to inscribe them for another year in the Book of Life.

For once he was listening. Over a week or more, during

those tremulous days between Rosh Hashanah and Yom Kippur, the so-called Days of Awe, practically all of Denmark's endangered Jews – nearly 6000 in toto – were ferried across the Oresund to Sweden. There they sought refuge with strangers or, better yet, relatives. Among them was Mrs Oberg's cousin and her two daughters. Mrs Oberg felt obligated to offer them shelter – she could do no other – despite her misgivings about the politics of Stig and Arnie. She had not seen her cousin – whose married name was Louise Brandes – for thirty years. But as young girls they had played together every summer on the beaches of Gotland. Mrs Oberg had no siblings, so Louise was, in effect, the custodian of her childhood memories. Only she could confirm the accuracy of her recollections of endless hours on the shores of the Baltic; picnics of crayfish and vodka (the latter for adults only, save for an occasional sip); long walks in cool pine forests. But she also recalled, unless she was mistaken, a disharmonious rivalry between her mother and Louise's (who was married to her mother's brother). She once overheard Louise's mother tell her own:

"It's a pity that Liv is such a plain child. But you must not give up hope. Look how Hans Christian Andersen's 'The Ugly Duckling' turned out."

Mrs Oberg longed to hear what Louise could add to those long-gone days, which now seemed as distant as the exile in Babylon, but she also dreaded her judgement:

"How could you, a Jew, have raised two Nazis?"

Mother and daughters were due on the overnight train from Kiruna, and Mrs Oberghad volunteered to collect them from the station. She recognized her relative at once.

"Welcome to Uppsala," she said.

The cousins embraced, and introductions were made. Liv

and Louise were separated by no more than six months. Likewise their own offspring were of compatible ages, as if they had procreated in co-ordination; the older now being 19, the younger 13. Further introductions were made over the dinner table, when Stig returned from work, and Arnie from his football practice. Until that moment the boys had no idea they were expecting dinner guests, let alone refugees from Denmark.

"Boys," said their mother, "this is my cousin Louise Brandes, and her daughters, Karen and Ella. Be nice."

Another surprise to the boys was the location of the meal. The Obergs usually dined in the kitchen, but on this occasion the dining room table had been spread with a cloth, the candelabra was alight with flaming candles, and crystal glasses had been filled from the one bottle of French wine the family owned. The dinner was not so formal as to have a seating plan, but Stig found himself beside Karen, and Arnie next to Ella. The hope being that the stories the girls had to tell of life under the Nazis might soften the world-view of her own boys.

"Tell me," said Stig, by way of an opening remark, "how exactly are we related?"

"Your mother and my mother are first cousins," said Karen.

"Meaning that you and I have one set of great grandparents in common," said Stig.

He did a rapid calculation and worked out that his own mother was likely Jewish. This was more than he could assimilate, given his standing in the Swedish Nazi party.

"Why did you never tell me that I had Jewish blood?" he said.

"It was of no relevance," said Mr Oberg, "until you fell

under Hitler's spell. Our initial response was to avoid embarrassing you. Now we can see that it was a mistake, for which we apologize."

Arnie took the revelation with greater composure – or seemed to – perhaps because for a teenager self-disgust is the norm. At the invitation of Mr Oberg, Louise Brandes spelled out the atrocious fate her family and the rest of Danish Jewry had so narrowly escaped: it began with transportation to the east in cattle cars, and ended in institutions beyond nightmare, where an attempt was being made to exterminate the Jewish race.

"They have a collective name," said Mrs Brandes, "death camps."

"And where," said Stig, looking around the table, "is Mr Brandes? On the run? Or on the way to some imaginary hell-hole?"

"My father is trapped in the United States," said Karen indignantly. "He went to give a series of lectures on Scandinavian drama, and found that he couldn't get home."

"Oh such places exist all right, of that you can be sure," said Mr Oberg, entering with the gravadlax, "and were the Nazis ever to invade Sweden you would find out the truth of the matter soon enough."

"But I am on their side," said Stig.

"Maybe you can be a Nazi and a Swede," said his father, serving the visitors first, "but you cannot be both a Nazi and a Jew. Not if you want to remain who you are."

"You sound like Polonius," said Stig, as if that were necessarily a bad thing.

"Please explain," said Mrs Brandes, "just what you have got against your own people?"

Stig snorted at the suggestion.

"Jews manage economies, enslave workers, start wars, and essentially control the machinery of the world," he said.

"If that is the case," said his father, "why do they need a God?"

****

Fortunately October proved to be warmer than the welcome, and during the afternoons and evenings there was still light enough for family outings. True, Stig continued to question the existence of Auschwitz, but he could hardly deny the existence of Karen, nor the effect it was having upon him. Being a Nazi was a matter of opinion, but the desire to mate was a biological imperative. Of course Stig fought against it, as was his duty, but he might just as well have tried to bottle the wind. Nor was Arnie immune; hormones were bounding through his veins like rabbits. One evening Stig suggested they all drive out to Gamla Upsala to see the three burial mounds beneath the generous glow of a full moon.

"You know what," said Ella, taking Arnie's arm in the dare-devil light, "we are not so closely related that we cannot marry."

Whereupon Arnie kissed her. Because she was the first girl he had ever kissed, he immediately thought himself in love. This, along with his Jewishness, was another secret to keep from his fellow Young Hitlerites. He still liked being a Nazi, but all of a sudden he liked being Arnie Oberg even more.

A new rhythm of co-existence was established in the apartment on Kyrkogardsgatan. Ella had been accepted at Arnie's school, Eriksskolan, to which they walked every morning arm-in-arm, while Karen found a job at the Carolina

Rediviva, indexing Danish periodicals, paying special attention to those produced clandestinely. Meanwhile the grown-up cousins shopped, cleaned, cooked, and co-ordinated memories. On a Sunday, early in January, as the snow fell silently outside, the two families sat around the pot-bellied stove, reading the weekend papers. What caught Mr Oberg's eye in particular was a report in the Norrkopings Tidningar about a new production of *The Merchant of Venice* at the Royal Dramatic Theatre in Stockholm. According to its director – Alf Sjoberg – it was an "indirect but poignant political gesture", designed to present Shylock as a "timeless and sympathetic representative of the Jewish race". Mr Oberg remembered the production of Hamlet at Elsinore, and wondered if this one might not produce an equal but opposite effect.

****

In any event he saw no reason not to book tickets for everyone. Even Stig agreed to come, having learned that Karen was too. Somehow he managed to maintain an equilibrium between his romantic interest in her, and his continuing infatuation with Nazism.

"Let's make this a proper outing," said Mrs Oberg.

But when they all met up Stig was sporting his formal Nazi attire, including red and black swastika armbands.

"Likely they'll lynch you," said Mr Oberg, "and I won't lift a finger to stop them."

"Is this your idea of compromise?" said Karen.

"I'm coming, aren't I?" said Stig.

Eventually he backed down, though he insisted upon retaining his conspicuous brown shirt. That crisis resolved they all latched themselves together like mountaineers, and slithered over icy pavements towards the station without anyone breaking a bone. The great theatre stood in a cupboard of light, as if the street beneath it were ablaze. There were already ticket-holders within, whispering to one another. Apparently they knew something Mr Oberg did not. He began to wonder if the King of Sweden might be in attendance. But no one in the theatre bar was any wiser than he. The auditorium, darkening as they took their seats, was suddenly cut by the rays of a massive spotlight, which finally settled on some characters near the front. At the same time Holger Lowenadler – the actor cast as Shylock – appeared before the curtains in propria persona.

"Tonight we are honoured by the presence of three special guests," he said, "survivors of Sasha Pechersky's revolt or escape – call it what you will – from Sobibor."

Everyone in the theatre, from the gods to the stalls, rose to offer these heroes a standing ovation. Everyone, that is, except for Stig.

"Show me the proof," he said, "and I'll stand soon enough."

Neither Ella nor Arnie had seen the play before, and both were mesmerized by Shylock who – unusually – eschewed an Ashkenazi or Sephardi accent, and spoke like a regular Swede. Even though his words were new to them, both joined the chorus of approval that greeted Shylock's most famous lines: "Hath not a Jew?" Even more emotion was generated by the trial scene, continually punctuated by onstage rowdies, clearly modeled after members of the Hitler Youth, and thereby meant to draw a parallel between Venice and – let's say – Berlin. As Shylock made his final exit from the courtroom, with everything gone bar his life, the audience once again offered a standing ovation, not only for the actor, it seemed, but for the people he was representing. While the cheering continued the spotlight swung from row to row, finally settling – once more – on the messengers from Sobibor. That night the happy ending – required by comedy – seemed almost an insult.

After Mr Lowenadler had taken his final curtain call one of the men from Sobibor approached Stig.

"Are you a cripple?" he said.

"No," said Stig.

"Then why are you not standing?" said the man. "And why are you wearing that fucking brown shirt?"

"Because I am a Nazi," said Stig.

Whereupon – without another word – the man slapped him across the cheek as hard as he was able.

"You're lucky that's all he did," said Mr Oberg. Stig did not know what to do first; wipe the tears from his eyes, or the blood from his nose.

"Looks like you have reached a crossroads," said Karen. "You have to decide: is it me that you love, or is it Hitler? You cannot continue to love us both."

"You could make a start," said Mr Oberg, "by conceding the existence of Sobibor."

For a moment Stig hesitated, then he buttoned his jacket to hide his brown shirt. Karen yelped with relief, and hugged her not-so-distant cousin. Arnie immediately felt the expectation for him to do the same. But he was tongue-tied by his brother's unexpected volte-face. It was all very well for him to renounce Nazism, but with what was he going to replace it? Kissing girls was not enough. He felt the eyes of everyone upon him, especially Ella's, but still he could not speak.

That night Arnie had a nightmare. Once more the family was driving towards Elsinore. They were near enough to see its battlements, and the Danish flag flying above them. Then there was a period of unaccountable time, and instead of sitting beside his mother in the car, Arnie found himself wandering on foot and alone. Trying to find his way he came upon a dead-end path blocked by super-abundant brambles. There was a rustling in the undergrowth, and a wild feline emerged. A handsome creature, more fitting to Stockholm Zoo, than the Scandinavian countryside. If anything it resembled a sabre-toothed tiger. Even as Arnie was contemplating its rare beauty, it leapt upon his chest, sank its horrid teeth into his tongue, and bit deeply. Asleep or not Arnie could still feel the pain of it. In fact it was bad enough to wake him up.

"What's the matter?" said his brother.

When Arnie didn't reply, Stig added: "Cat got your tongue?"

A WILDERNESS OF MONKEYS

AFTER THE WAR the Belmont could hardly declare itself Judenrein, but certain signs made it clear that Jews were not welcome at the hotel. Only in 1961, after the trial of Eichmann in Jerusalem, was the unofficial ban relaxed, to be replaced by a quota.The Salmons were one of seven Jewish families accommodated that summer. Their journey to Venice turned out to be unexpectedly traumatic: over the Alps the BEA Viscount in which they flew encountered clear-air turbulence, so bad that stewardesses tumbled and the overhead lockers burst open spilling bags upon the helpless passengers; some screamed, others bled. David Salmon looked as if he were a screamer, but no sound came from his mouth. In fact he was retching, but his efforts were to no avail; producing neither vomit nor relief. Motion sickness continued to shake him to the core, just as clear air turbulence was rattling the plane. His wife – Beth – seeing her husband's body shudder uncontrollably and his face turn puce, began to fear that his heart was failing and cried out for help. A stewardess answered her call on her hands and knees, but the best she could offer was smelling salts and a half-spilled glass of water. The boys – Calman and Leon – had never before contemplated the possibility of a dead parent. Neither liked the idea. As suddenly as it had begun the turmoil ceased. But Beth Salmon could not put it behind her. She knew it was an omen, but of what she knew not.

Fortunately the ride in the vaporetto from the airport to the Belmont's private landing restored her husband's normal colour; his appetite too, as his grumbling stomach testified. When they entered the grand hotel with its long wings and high central tower they couldn't help but notice the excessive number of carabinieri in the reception area and the grounds.

"Probably has something to do with the Film Festival," said Salmon, a keen moviegoer. "Perhaps someone like Gina Lollobrigida is about to arrive."

"You should be so lucky," said his wife.

"It is true that we are anticipating the presence of several film stars," confirmed the receptionist, "but the carabinieri are not present because of them. No, signore, no. They are here because last night our establishment drew the attention of a notorious cat burglar. Such visitations are unfortunate, but to be expected when you welcome as many wealthy guests as we do."

****

"Best lock the french windows before we go to eat," said Salmon, as he collected his sons.

The maître'd accosted the party at the restaurant's entrance.

"You have a reservation?" he said.

He wore a tuxedo, and his hair rose and fell like corrugated steel.

"We are guests," said Salmon.

"Are you familiar with our dress code?" said the maître'd. "No service without a jacket and tie. You seem to have neither."

"It is our first night," said Salmon, "and it is getting late."

"In the circumstances I am prepared to make an exception," said the maître'd, "provided none of the other diners objects."

The Salmons looked at their judges through the sealed glass doors. All appeared as though they had stepped out of the pages of a fashion magazine. They sat around tables furnished with items rarely seen at the Salmons: napery, starched and white; silver condiment sets; and breathing bottles of wine. There was laughter, and the music of glasses being filled, tapped and emptied. Cigarette smoke hung in the air like the vapour trails of spontaneous wit.

Seated apart at a table nearest the glass door was a Contessa and a Chihuahua, though the latter was actually squatting on the table. Both were eating from the same plate. The Chihuahua of course was naked. The Contessa's pink evening wear perhaps by Dior – revealed large patches of mummified skin and matched her hair. Around her neck was a crucifix constructed from blue diamonds. She was holding something to her eyes; not a lorgnette but mother-of-pearl opera glasses. They were trained on the Salmons. Obviously she didn't take to what she saw, because she began to hiss like a goose. Her agitation caused a faint miasma of rouge to drift upwards from her cheeks. The maître'd approached her table, and leaned his ear towards her mouth.

Returning he said: "I am sorry. You cannot enter. Already there has been an objection."

****

It had been a moonless night when the Salmons pitched up at the Belmont. Rising soon after the sun both boys stood on their little terrace and beheld the revelation darkness had withheld: a desert that glowered like gold dust, an oasis of thatched parasols and wooden huts, and an irresistible mirage that resembled a painted sea.

Rousing their parents in the adjacent room they demanded: "When can we go to the beach?"

"Not today," said their father. "Patience is *le mot du jour*: today we are destined to enrich the merchants of Venice."

The boys looked like a poster for *Paradise Lost*.

"Don't stare at me like that," said their father, "it's not my fault. Blame your mother."

Returning to Room 408 after their humiliation by the maître'd, Beth had noted the paucity of the evening wear they had packed – one suit for him, one gown for her – and declared it woefully inadequate for a fortnight's stay at the Belmont.

"What will they think of us," she had said, "if we show up in the same outfits night after night? Remember we are representing not only ourselves, but – in the eyes of those goyim – our people also."

"How can they possibly know that we are Jews?" said Salmon. "That bitch with the Chihuahua, she knew all right," said Beth.

****

The first items they acquired were jackets for the boys at a haberdashers right on St Mark's Square. Salmon, after flicking through the rack of ready-made suits, picked out half-a-dozen to try on, two of which passed Beth's inspection (she liked the Egyptian cotton, and the silk, but thought the wool impractical and the mohair horribly vulgar). He bought both.

Inspired by the Diors and the Chanels being displayed in the Belmont's forbidden zone, Beth tracked down a couturier near the Rialto who had near identical copies of not simply Dior and Chanel, but also Simonetta, Balenciaga and Schiaparelli. She had a good figure, which the dresses pulled out by the shop assistant only enhanced. Even her sons could see that. The fittings had an uncanny effect upon them, suggesting that their mother might have – or rather, have had – a more important existence outside of the home. That they might, in some inadvertent way, have clipped her wings. But there was no sign of any such thing as she departed the shop with a package that contained an ersatz Simonetta, an ersatz Schiaparelli, and a near-perfect Dior clone.

With more to buy the Salmons meandered down alleys, crossed bridges, and explored arcades, including the Procuratie Nuove, which seemed to consist entirely of jewellery stores. In one, with the unlikely name of Giurovich, Beth tried on a necklace of pearly glass faceted to resemble diamonds.

"Nice," said her husband.

"That's not why I'm going to buy it," said Beth, "I want to use it to strangle that bloody woman's dwarf dog."

Eventually the Salmons homed in on the Ghetto, entering it through one of the original gateways. The gates themselves were long-gone of course, but the posts remained, as did the giant worm-holes left by the screws that fixed the hinges. Each clutching packages, all wrapped in brown paper, the family created the false impression that they were refugees – all worldly goods in hand – seeking sanctuary from persecution. Or perhaps the impression wasn't so accidental after all.

"Listen Calman, listen Leon," said Salmon, as Beth disappeared into an aromatic shop that promised *dolci ebraici*, "our family might not have come from this Ghetto, but it certainly came from another. My father – God rest his soul – grew up in the Ukraine, and your mother's – God rest his – in Poland. Alas, even in England they found no rest; on the contrary, they worked themselves to an early grave – the one peddling second-hand shoes from a push-cart, the other altering suits in a sweatshop – so that their children, and their children's children might lead better lives. And we do, don't we? Instead of some lice-infested tenement in the East End, we've just moved into a nice house in Hendon, and Calman had a wonderful barmitzvah at the Café Royal – at least your mother and I thought so – all of which makes it so much more important never to forget the sacrifices of your ancestors."

As though in search of those mislaid individuals Salmon strode across the Campo Ghetto Nuovo, opened the imposing green door of the Casa Israelitica di Riposo as if it were his own, and ushered his boys inside.

Before Beth had a chance to catch up with her family, Salmon singled out Calman and whispered: "I am going to disappear for thirty minutes. Tell your mother I left my wallet in one of the shops – I'm pretty certain which – and that I have gone to retrieve it. Wait for me here."

Calman did as he was commanded, but Beth looked mystified. Her expression remained unchanged as she opened a paper bag marked *Panificio Bassi* and offered the messenger a *bisse*, a biscuit shaped like the letter S or perhaps a snake. Meanwhile a man in his thirties emerged from the only office in view, presumably the Casa's director. He was wearing his jacket in a rakish style, as if it were a cape. It created the illusion, if only for a second, that he had four arms. Such was his welcome that the remaining Salmons felt embraced by all of them.

He led them along a hallway, through a library, and into a garden, scented by lilac and shaded by sweet chestnuts. About twenty residents were in various states of animation; some argued, some studied *La Repubblica* or read sensational paperbacks, most slumbered. Having known only their mother's mother, Calman and Leon were unaccustomed to the elderly, and to be among them was not their idea of fun, especially when there was a perfect alternative on the Lido. As it turned out, the director could read their minds.

"The lives of these men and women have not been easy ones," he said. "To your ears Mussolini may sound like a forbidden dish of spaghetti and shellfish, but to them he was the man who turned their world upside-down. A little over twenty years ago he enacted legislation – called the racial laws – that made them – and all other Jews – strangers in their own land. Many lost their livelihoods, and – imagine this – in the summer they were banned from the Lido."

"At last," said Beth, "something my boys can identify with."

"And that was just the start of their troubles," said the director.

He looked at Calman.

"When were you born?" he said.

"1948," said the boy.

"Just four years before your birth," said the director, "a detachment of SS troops – and 'detachment' is the perfect collective noun – raided this place and took away twenty-two men and women, all of whom perished en route or at Auschwitz. Altogether 205 Venetian Jews were seized by the

SS. Just eight returned. You are looking at some of those survivors."

****

That evening as they rode the vaporetto to the Lido with Venice at their backs, Salmon resembled a man who had not only found his wallet, but also the key to the Doge's safe. What was going on? His wife no longer looked mystified; she appeared frankly suspicious.

Soon, however, more serious considerations drove those suspicions out of her mind. From a vantage point at the end of Leon's bed Beth supervised the boys as they dressed for dinner. She knotted their ties, fastened the middle buttons on their brand-new jackets, and flattened their hair with tap-water. Examining her handiwork she licked her finger and wiped a smudge from Calman's cheek.

"Perfect," she said.

Her own ensemble was also pretty startling. She had chosen the Dior – well, the one next door to Dior – which began at her bust, leaving her shoulders quite bare. Around her throat were the glass beads from Giurovich. The dress remained hemmed in till her waist, from where it cascaded freely to the floor. Salmon opted for the Egyptian cotton. If not movie stars they could have passed for a producer and his trophy wife. They strode from the elevator and marched upon the Belmont's dining room, sweeping aside the fawning maître'd. The watchful Contessa was rendered mute. Beth noticed with satisfaction that the Chihuahua gulped when it glimpsed her fiery necklace. Heads undoubtedly turned as they were led to their table. Calman, who was studying *King Lear* in school, wondered if any of the lascivious Italians were echoing King Lear's infamous declaration: "But to the girdle do the gods inherit; beneath is all the fiends'."

Having gained admittance to the exclusive area the pity was that the Salmons could not enjoy the fruits of their invasion. But they were not adventurous eaters. Beth's stomach possessed an on-board rabbi briefed to detect immediately any infringement of the laws of kashrut. The sanctions were not pleasant to behold. And so, instead of steak tartare, beef carpaccio, octopus, oysters, or mussels, they ordered Dover sole; instead of champagne or prosecco they asked for San Pelligrino and Coca Cola (without ice).

Having survived the main course – conservative it may have been, but it was cooked in a continental kitchen – they were considering dessert when they heard a collective intake of breath, and saw a tall woman approaching their table. She was clearly not a waitress.

"Oh my God," said Salmon, "that's what's-her-name – it's on the tip of my tongue – the starlet who appeared topless at Cannes, caught the eye of Vittorio Da Sica, and got herself cast as a voluptuous shepherdess in the Festival's hottest ticket; the *Bandits of Orgosolo*. What can she want with us?"

He remained blind to the fact that her evening gown was in every respect identical to his wife's, except that it was genuine. The coincidence was not lost on Beth, who sat transfixed. Arriving at the table the woman's dramatic gestures made it apparent that she was inviting her new-found twin to arise. Beth obliged and felt the newcomer's eyes upon her. The woman made no effort to introduce herself. Instead she delivered a lament that touched Beth on account of its passionate vehemence and obvious sincerity. Had she grasped its meaning she would likely have felt otherwise.

"Tonight an important new movie in which I feature

prominently will have its premiere at the Festival," said the woman. "For the occasion I am wearing a gown made exclusively for me – just for me – by Christian Dior. And what do I find? Only that this interloper has stolen my moment, robbed me of my joy. This is the thanks we get for letting Jews into the Belmont. How can we assimilate thieves? Impossible! They may copy us, but they will never be like us. They should be in the ghetto, where they belong."

Having run out of words she flounced out of the dining room, supported by her escort, each step attended by sympathetic glances or raised glasses.

"Whatever she said," noted Salmon, "it didn't seem very sisterly."

****

In the morning Calman and Leon watched as their father threaded a roll of Kodachrome 8mm into the body of his brand new Bolex movie camera. On the beach the in-and-out of the Adriatic sounded like a paintbrush in perpetual motion, while the camera resembled a clock, one whose tick-tock marked an investment in future time, a small deposit in the familial memory bank (each roll lasting approximately four minutes). Salmon was filming when little Leon ran down to the water clutching his inflatable green canoe beneath his right arm. He shot Beth as she smeared Ambre Solaire on her shoulders, and Calman – wrapped in a blue dressing-gown – as he sequestered himself on the porch of their cabana.

A lip-reader could probably make out Beth's words as she registered that her older boy was hiding from the sun like a vampire: "For God's sake, Calman, come out of the shadows and get yourself a tan. You want people to think you went to the North Pole for your summer holiday?"

Like many mothers Beth was a nag, and probably repeated the order numerous times. Calman ignored it, and continued reading Dostoyevsky. Salmon's camera went on ticking, preserving memories that would likely outlast the participants, assuming that celluloid is more durable than flesh, so that strangers might one day pick up the film (coiled around its little spool) at some inner city market and wonder who all the people were, and what happened to them afterwards. As a matter of fact, something big did happen that very night.

****

August 16 was David and Beth's wedding anniversary.

"Let's make it a night to remember," said Salmon, "let's show those snooty goyim the real meaning of class."

He persuaded his wife of twenty years to wear the Simonetta, which was emerald green, and cut even lower than the Dior (though it did have shoulder straps). For himself he chose the suit of midnight blue.

Before the family descended to the dining room, Salmon summoned Calman and Leon to Room 408. It was then that he finally revealed the cause of the Mona Lisa smile that had so unsettled Beth. Inserting a hand deep into the side-pocket of his suitcase, he pulled forth – with all the aplomb of a magician – a box some 12 inches long. He handed it to Beth. She pressed a little button and its lid sprang open.

"Are you crazy?" she said. "How can we afford something like this?"

"The factory," said Salmon. "People are building houses by the hundreds, and they need furniture. Lots of it."

"It's still too expensive," said Beth.

"Nonsense," said Salmon. "According to the Book of Proverbs the price of a virtuous woman is far above rubies – far above – in which case this is nothing more than a deposit."

Lost for words, Beth wept.

"If I remember correctly these are some of the qualities of a virtuous woman," continued Salmon. "The heart of her husband doth safely trust in her. She will do him good and not evil all the days of her life. She is like the merchants' ships; she bringeth food from afar. Or at least from Vivian Avenue."

Calman and Leon were in unfamiliar territory, the pays inconnu of adult emotion, so they were relieved at the introduction of a familiar landmark. Vivian Avenue, Hendon, was where they shopped: at Martin's the all-purpose grocer; at Graber's the delicatessen (for herring and pickles straight from the barrel); at Grodzinski the baker (for cholla and beigels); and at Carmelli the fruiterer (with the meshuga owner). Strangely enough the ruby necklace, now luminescent in his mother's cupped hands, reminded Calman of nothing so much as a pound of fresh stewing steak from Leslie Mann, the famous kosher butcher, also of Vivian Avenue. Though when Salmon secured it around Beth's neck it looked like a million dollars.

The maître'd almost bowed when he saw them, but didn't quite. The Contessa, however, went all the way. She scrutinized the Salmons with her opera glasses as they progressed through the dining room, then – in this order – she screamed and swooned face-down into her *spaghetti al burro* (with *salsa pomodoro*). Her companion stopped eating and barked. The maître'd rushed to her side, lifted her head, and gently tapped her cheeks, raising so much rouge as to almost alter the climate in the dining room. It certainly felt frosty around the table where the Salmons sat.

Before their first course – *minestra vegetariana* – was delivered it was surrounded by carabinieri. Even worse than seeing their parents overcome by emotion was the vision of them trapped in a situation beyond their control. Calman only had to observe his father's newly acquired tan suddenly vanish to know that he was scared. Two waiters appeared ferrying the soup, but the maître'd motioned them away with a flick of his wrist.

"The Contessa has made a serious accusation," he announced. "According to her the rubies presently adorning your wife's neck were – until the day before yesterday – her property. She thinks you are the notorious cat burglar."

"Impossible," said Salmon, "two days ago I wasn't even in Italy."

"No one seriously believes that someone like you could be a cat burglar," said the maître'd, "but it is suspected that you are – how to say it? – a receiver of stolen property. A lesser crime, but a crime nonetheless."

The silence that followed was broken by one of the carabinieri who demanded – none too politely – that Beth surrender the disputed property. She tried. But her hands were shaking so violently that – try as she might – she was unable to release the clasp. She looked at her older son.

"Would you mind, Calman?" she said.

The back of her neck felt frighteningly hot to the boy, hotter even than the alleged contraband. As Beth passed the rubies over to the authorities, she looked at her husband.

"What have you done?" she said.

Salmon had no chance to explain himself because, at that moment, two carabinieri plucked him from his chair and frog-marched him out of the dining room. As soon as the doors had shut behind him the maître'd raised his arm and waved, a gesture so discreet as to be almost invisible. Nonetheless two waiters answered his summons, this time with only three soup bowls.

"Are they out of their minds?" said Beth. "How can we eat after what just happened?"

They were already rising to leave when a man – not quite a stranger – took Salmon's vacant seat. Calman recognised him first, by his jacket's empty sleeves.

"Please spare a moment to listen," he said. "It could be important, I think. My name is Italo Calevi. We met two days ago at the Casa di Riposo. My father is an *avvocato*, a lawyer. Everyone in Venice knows his name. I fear you are going to require his skills."

****

Salmon would certainly have seconded that opinion. But he was dumbstruck by circumstance. Without protest he was bundled into the back of a van marked *Polizia Penitenziaria* and transported to Santa Bona prison in Treviso, a journey of some forty minutes. The door to his cell was painted ultramarine, but no colour – however bright – could disguise the fact that it was made of iron. Still in a state of shock he curled up on a stale mattress in the corner and – as the iron door was slammed shut upon him – prepared for a long night in his single-occupancy ghetto.

Morning arrived for Salmon, sleep-deprived and

unshaven, at around 7.00 am, when the cell door was reopened to admit a man who introduced himself as Beppo Calevi.

"As Portia was to Antonio," he said, "so am I to you."

He was carrying a briefcase and a bent-wood chair, upon which he sat. Salmon raised himself, in person, and – ever-so-slightly – in spirit.

"I have pulled a few strings," said Calevi, "and have secured you a hearing at the Tribunale later today. Perhaps by then the Ministerio pubblico will have discovered that the *parte lesa* – the injured party – is subject to hysterical outbursts – especially when in the company of Jews – and thrown out the accusation *perché il fatto non sussiste* – because the crime did not take place. Against that we know the cat burglar is a reality, and that he did rob several guests at the Belmont. If it turns out that your accuser actually was one of his victims, and is indeed missing a ruby necklace, then of course you will plead *non colpevole* – not guilty – and I will do the rest."

****

Giuseppe Montefiore was still asleep when Beppo Calevi called him at 9.30.

"You have driven me from the world of dreams," he said "and flung me into the gulag of the everyday. You are like – what are they called?"

"A Philistine?" said Calevi.

"No, no," said Montefiore, "like the man from Porlock, the man who woke Coleridge from his dream of Xanadu. Compared to mine that was but a puff of smoke. It began in the small hours when I dropped off after a few drinks – you know what I mean by a 'few' – and was captivated by such a vision that I thought – even in my sleep – 'I must remember this'. But then I needed to take a piss, and by the time I got back to my bed I had forgotten everything. I went to sleep again in hope of revisiting that lost continent. As the second dream progressed I joined a group of drinkers in an ornamental garden. They looked like good company. 'Who are you?' I said. 'Who are we?' they replied. 'Why, we are the people from the dream you forgot.' Now – thanks to you – I will never remember who they were. Why are you bothering me so early, you bastard?"

Like Calevi, Montefiore had studied law, but unlike his friend had abandoned his studies after a couple of years. He could have been a star of the legal system; instead he became a fixer, whose dominion was the shadows.

"Giuseppe, old boy," said Calevi, "there's been some unpleasantness at the Belmont. An English tourist has been detained, on suspicion of being an accomplice of the cat burglar. His name is David Salmon; mid-forties; married with two boys; and he's a Jew. He needs you to fix things. *Presto, presto.*"

Monteflore began by interviewing the family in Room 408. But Beth was too angry, and Leon too young; only Calman impressed him.

"Dad heard there were rumours that Orson Welles might show up at the Film Festival with his version of Kafka's *The Trial*," he said. "Little did he realize that he would be starring in it."

"Don't you worry," said Montefiore, "there won't be a trial. I'm here to fix things."

Beth laughed.

"We're not talking about a sink with a leak," she said.

****

Montefiore escorted Beth and the boys to Santa Lucia and put them on the train to Treviso, with instructions to take a taxi to the Palazzo di Giustizia at the other end. The platform was crowded, as was the train. Calman stuck his head out of the window, just before it departed. Seeing him Montefiore spread his arms wide, as if to encompass the entire railway station.

"The world is full of people who don't know they haven't been born," he shouted. "Of course they are invisible, but they don't know that either. Sometimes I suspect I am one of them. Perhaps that's why I am such a good fixer."

"Don't be silly," said Calman, "I can see you."

But the very next moment Montefiore was obscured by a cloud of steam that rose from beneath the carriage as the train prepared to leave the station.

****

Salmon would certainly have elected to be among the invisible when he spied his wife and sons seated in the front row of the public gallery. But he could hardly ignore Calman and Leon's demonstration of loyalty, a coalition that apparently did not include Beth, who acted as if he were a stranger. He acknowledged his family with an appropriately modest gesture, and took his place beside his lawyer. The proceedings were conducted in Italian, of course, but you didn't need to be a linguistor even a semiotician to deduce a happy outcome. The way Salmon leaped up and embraced his lawyer after the *Giudice per le Indagini Preliminari* had delivered his opinion made it sufficiently obvious. Calevi later explained that he had presented his client as a wealthy industrialist, with no criminal history, who had acquired the rubies in good faith. He added that the Contessa was equally beyond reproach, but alas subject to the infirmities of age. Moreover, he had concluded, it was yet to be ascertained whether the rubies Salmon had gifted to his wife were the same as the ones the Contessa had allegedly lost. In response to which the GIP – in Calevi's free translation – had ruled that his client was to remain an *indagato* – a suspect – pending further investigations by the *Ministerio pubblico*, that he was prohibited from leaving the country, and that he was to remain under house arrest at the Belmont.

Beppo Calevi was required to stay on in Treviso, having other clients to represent, but he summoned a taxi to return the others to Venice. Salmon sat in front beside the driver. Although exhausted and hungry he felt strangely elated, as though he had already been acquitted. Beth, in the back with the boys, maintained her vow of silence, while exhaling hot gusts of ire. The road was long and straight, the fields on either side filled with unfamiliar crops. Speaking pidgin Italian, Salmon asked the driver to identify them. Turning to face his family he repeated what he had learned.

"The farmers in this region," he said, "are famed for growing hoovers and mice."

The absurdity of the image detonated the tension, and the boys bubbled over with delighted cackles. And even though Beth knew that "mice" was a garbling of the Italian for rice, and that "uvas" were grapes, she elected to withhold the information, and – despite herself – joined in the laughter. If only someone had thought to bring the Bolex.

****

When it came to dinner Beth insisted upon room service.

Addressing her husband she said: "How you can even think of showing your face in the dining room is beyond me."

He said: "Because I am innocent."

"Are you so sure?" said Beth.

"You are kidding?" said Salmon.

"I wish I were," said Beth. "But I know you too well. You'd trust Satan if he gave you his word. I imagine you thought you'd got a great bargain when you picked up those rubies at some fly-by-night kiosk on the Rialto. Some bargain! It has cost us our good name. And maybe your freedom. Not to mention the damage done to your sons."

She recalled that inscrutable smile of his, and felt like screaming.

Dinner, when it came, was eaten in silence, a silence only broken by the unexpected arrival of Montefiore. He beckoned Salmon to the balcony.

"Sometimes my best work is done in my sleep," he said. "Last night, for example, I had this dream that I am only now beginning to understand. It wasn't the sort of dream I can discuss in front of women and children, because it involved my prick, which – I can tell you – kept getting longer and longer and longer. In fact it got so long that it bounded out of the house and into the street like a python. I chased after it – as if I were some figure in a cartoon – but it kept bouncing out of reach. People jeered, calling my penis a prothesis, and a fake. They threw stones at it, and it began to shed droplets of blood. I looked around for a place to hide. Then I spotted a small window. On the other side of the glass two women were watching; one was the Contessa, the other your wife."

Montefiore ceased his volcanic utterances and looked towards the heavens, where long clouds were braided with copper and gold, a detail lost on Salmon.

"If I were your shrink I'd have a comment or two," he said, "but as I am your client I have none. Tell me, what has all this Freudian nonsense to do with my case?"

"I understand," said Montefiore, "you do not have the time to be patient. So let me put it this way: Sherlock Holmes had Dr Watson, and I have my prick. It often tells me things, without knowing what they signify. It's my job – being the brains – to work out what's what. The first thing I thought about, after I opened my eyes, were those droplets of blood. What did they signify? Rubies, of course. Maybe even a necklace made of them. A necklace that properly belonged to one of the women behind the window. Both could not be telling the truth. Or could they? Then I remembered what my detractors had been shouting: *falso, falso*; fake, fake."

****

The following afternoon Montefiore somehow convened a mock trial in the Belmont's dining room, between the lunch and dinner sittings. The maître'd agreed to sit in as the *Giudice*, the judge. As well as the Salmons, the Contessa and her familiar were also present. Montefiore had but one witness to call, the jeweller Giurovich.

"Contessa," said Montefiore, "are you absolutely certain that your rubies are the real thing?"

"Are you wishing to insult me," she said. "Of course they are authentic."

Montefiore turned to Giurovich.

“An introduction to rubies, if you please,” he said.

“Our own Marco Polo described a ruby as the most resplendent object upon earth,” said the expert witness, “with a value so great that a price for it in money could hardly be named at all. These days the best stones come from the valley of Mogok in Burma. When cut they are the colour of pigeon’s blood. The ancients believed they contained an unquenchable fire. If you shine a light on a Mogok stone you can see why.”

“Are the rubies in this necklace from Mogok?” said Montefiore.

“No,” said the jeweller. “They are not even rubies. In my opinion they are spinels. Most likely synthetic.”

“Spinels?” said the Contessa. “What are spinels?”

“Not rubies,” said Giurovich.

On hearing this the Contessa grabbed the necklace with her gnarled old hand and tossed it at Salmon.

“Here,” she said, “take your pound of flesh.”

Beth seemed equally angry.

“Isn’t that just like my husband?” she said. “To pay good money for a worthless fake.”

Even before the maître’d could pronounce the verdict of not guilty – *Perchè l’imputato non lo ha commesso* – Beppo Calevi suddenly burst through the glass doors followed by a brace of carabinieri.

They stood motionless for a moment, looking like a crooner and his backing singers.

“A miracle!” Calevi said at last. “The cat burglar has been captured, and the Contessa’s rubies recovered. I have them with me, hence my escort.”

Both necklaces were placed side-by-side on a white table-cloth and declared identical, at least until the beam of a torch was directed at them, whereupon only one seemed to catch fire. The case against Salmon was dropped. Beth later offered an apology. Neither Montefiore nor Calevi would accept a fee. The Contessa never said a word.

****

The Salmons spent most of their remaining days at the Belmont beneath cloudless blue skies, enjoying the exclusive privileges of its private beach. On the penultimate morning they arose in unison from their sun-loungers, hop-scotched across sand that scorched their soles as if it were some satanic pie-crust, and homed in on the African who rented out the pedallos. Salmon paired up with Beth, Calman with Leon. Having pedalled half-way to the Barbary Shore, husband and wife rotated, and Salmon scrutinized the Belmont through the viewfinder of his Bolex, as if he were Armand of Armand and Michaela Denis. He imagined that he was approaching the Lido for the very first time. How to explain the gigantic building that dominated the strand like some tin-pot dictator's folly? And who were those gilded figures cavorting in the silver-plated surf?

"Why," said Salmon, "this place is nothing but a wilderness of monkeys."

****

That afternoon they had arranged to revisit the Casa Israelitica di Riposo, to thank Italo Calevi for his invaluable assistance. Once there they all agreed to have coffee and Coca Colas in the Campo. A man of about Salmon's age, with well-cut grey hair and a clean white T-shirt cut a diagonal path towards their table. As he neared he began to shout at them like a man with Tourette's.

Calevi provided a rough translation: "From morning to night walking around here I see that you are a different race – a *razza di merda* – a race of shit."

The man cupped his head, in mockery of the kipa.

As if the suppressed anger of the last fortnight could no longer be withheld, Salmon jumped to his feet, approached the intruder, and punched him hard on the nose. It bled, and he staggered back, but he did not fall. It was Salmon who fell.

"Isn't that typical," said Beth. "My husband hits someone, and he's the one who falls down."

Salmon was on his knees now, and beginning to retch. His face was the colour of a lemon.

"Help me," he said. "The Ghetto is spinning."

Recognising that something life-threatening was underway, Beth changed her tune: she screamed. Calman and Leon watched both parents in terror. Calevi more usefully summoned a doctor from the Casa di Riposo, who diagnosed a heart attack.

"I knew something like this would happen," said Beth, as they bounced over the wavelets in the ambulance towards the Ospedale Civile.

All these events occurred many years ago, if not to me, then to someone very like me. Like Calman's father my own had his first heart attack in Venice, and his second – some thirty-five years later – when he revisited the city on a cruise liner. He used to joke that the doctors at the Ospedale Civile had saved his life, and the heart attack his marriage. By the time of his second he was already a widower. His heart stopped when he was playing bridge in the ship's lounge, and on this occasion no doctor was able to restart it. My brother and I decided to bury him in the Jewish cemetery on the Lido. Both Montefiore and Italo Calevi attended.

"I hope you hung on to the rubies," said Montefiore at the shiva.

"Actually we did," I said. "My mother refused to wear them, but my father cherished them – even though they were phoneys – as his ultimate deterrent, ready for use should my mother ever doubt him again."

"Good," said Montefiore.

"Why 'good'?" I said.

"Because I switched the necklaces," said Montefiore. "The Contessa got the fake."

I could hear my late mother's voice: "Serves the old bitch right."

"But why didn't you tell us before?" I said.

"Because it would have made of you accomplices," said Montefiore, "but now, I think, the statute of limitations has expired."

****

Every few years, on my father's yahrzeit, I return to say kaddish over his bones. On my most recent visit I bumped into Montefiore at the graveside. Though a few years younger than my father he must have been well into his nineties.

"Believe it or not, I still fix things for people," he said, "but there seems to be no one among the medical profession who can fix things for me. Nothing works, not even my prick. The other night I dreamed that it stood up like it used to do in better days. But it took one look at the unfamiliar landscape – said 'What am I doing here?' – and sank back down again. It is how it is."

We walked together – slowly – in the direction of the Belmont.

"You will be surprised how things have turned out," said Montefiore.

He was right. The cabanas and the thatched parasols were still there, but the beach was deserted, and the Belmont boarded up. A crane towered above it, like a giant gallows.

"It has been sold to Russians," said Montefiore, "who want to turn the old rooms into luxury apartments."

Although it was summer a cold wind blew down from the Dolomites, ruffling the Adriatic, and shifting the sand beneath our feet.

****

When I returned to England the TLS invited me to review Etgar Keret's new memoir, *Seven Good Years*. It was a quick read. The chapter on the death of his father stuck in my mind. I'll tell you why. Because it dawned on me that I was identifying not with the author but with the deceased. When had this happened? When had I ceased to share the son's POV? The questions gave me the willies. Although it was after midnight I dialed my father's old telephone number, just to see if I still remembered it. To my surprise a connection was made. After three rings someone answered. There was no mistaking the voice. This was no dream, Giuseppe, this really happened.

"Dad?" I said.

"Calman," said my father, "why are you phoning so late? Is something the matter?"

If You Tickle Us

BACK IN THE 1920s and 30s the Carps and the Salmons – immigrant families both – shared a house on Ellen Street, in London's East End. Abe Carp, the head of one family, trained boxers in a gym above a pub, including – as it turned out – his own son, while Simeon Salmon, the head of the other, was a cobbler of sorts. The families had something else in common, besides an address; both having been given their family names by ETA Hoffmann, who – as head of the Prussian civil service in Warsaw – was required to standardize Jewish patronymics, lest their bearers evade taxation and conscription. Even in this minute particular Hoffmann exercised his peculiar humour. Petitioners who turned up on Fridays were named after whatever fish was on the luncheon menu.

Like their aquatic namesakes, the Carps and the Salmons spawned numerous progeny, among them the greatest feather-weight of his generation, Izzy "Kid" Carp. Despite his father's profession the Kid had no inkling of his inner pugilist, until the day his PE teacher – an avowed Mosleyite – ordered him to go three rounds with the class bully. The goy's first blow made the Kid's nose bleed, the second split his lip, but the third never landed. Instead the Kid delivered a southpaw that caused the bully to reel, then tapped him lightly on the chin, and finally finished him off with a vicious wallop below the belt. The teacher cried "Foul", but then considered the repercussions of having pitted a feather-weight against a heavy-weight and closed the subject.

Izzy "Kid" Carp, however, became a regular in his father's gym, which turned out to be his university. Having graduated summa cum laude, he flawlessly boxed his way aged nineteen to the feather-weight championship of Great Britain, a day that saw Ellen Street criss-crossed with red, white and blue bunting. The Kid's contemporary, and unofficial twin, David Salmon, acted as his second throughout his brief career (curtailed by Hitler's war). Promotional photographs show the Kid with fists raised, a Mogen David provocatively embroidered on his baggy trunks. In the ring he was – it's fair to say – aggressively Jewish.

Not that he was noticeably passive outside it. At the famous Battle of Cable Street – when all of sixteen, and marching with the Labour League of Youth – he was so incensed by the cries of "Jew bastard" and "Go back to Palestine", that he knocked at least three Blackshirts out cold, and maybe – on this he was more equivocal – a couple of special constables.

Because Salmon sat in his corner during every bout, Carp felt obligated to attend his friend's occasional appearances at the Unity Theatre in St Pancras. These were not frequent because Salmon was officially a stagehand, whose acting skills were only called upon when an understudy was required. As it happened one was needed on the opening night of Ben Bengal's *Plant in the Sun*, an American play about working class solidarity. Salmon was laying out the costumes – dungarees mainly – when he received an urgent summons from its director, Herbert Marshall: would he be prepared to take on a small part – two lines, tops – at very short notice? The big thing was that its star was Paul Robeson. After the curtain calls Salmon asked Carp what it had been like.

"Like?" said Carp. "It was like watching Joe Louis fight."

****

In 1941 Salmon discovered a recording on the OKeh label of Paul Robeson – backed by the entire Count Basie Orchestra – singing King Joe, Parts 1 & 2. "I've been in Cleveland, St Louis, Chicago too," the conscripts sang, as if they really had, "but the best is Harlem when a Joe Louis fight is through."

They loved all things American, especially the movies. To them each one was a message from a distant – more attractive – planet. They often double-dated, taking girls to the Hackney Picturehouse on Mare Street. It was there that Salmon fell in love, not with any of his dates, but with Harpo, Groucho and Chico. Carp could never understand his friend's enthusiasm for the Marx Brothers. Such Lords of Misrule were all very well, but they were surely no match for the Iron Men of Berlin, Rome, and Madrid.

He preferred gangster movies, actually anything starring those diminutive Jewish tough guys; John Garfield, Paul Muni, and Edward G Robinson. Of the three Carp favoured Garfield, perhaps because he sometimes played boxers. Returning home from leave he would sneak into his parents bedroom, strip down to his underpants, pose before the family's only full-length mirror, and punch the air, always looking to see if he had captured Garfield's air of corrupted sweetness, his righteous belligerence. Izzy "Kid" Carp might have got himself killed on the Normandy beaches, but as John Garfield he was sure to survive D-day without a scratch.

David Salmon was married during the War – to a girl he met at the Unity – and Izzy "Kid" Carp shortly after V-E Day. Despite the head start, Carp's children were born first – in 1946 – Salmon's followed in 1948, and again in 1952, the year that both families took possession of semi-detacheds in Hendon.

****

"We should have named you Stalin and you Trotsky," said Carp to his boys, who could never agree on anything.

Not that their real names – Esau and Jacob – didn't smack of potential fratricide. They were called Esau and Jacob because they were twins, albeit non-identical. Even in the womb they had sparred, apparently vying for the right to be the firstborn, a bout Esau won.

When the twins grew sentient politics was added to pugilism, and the fights grew nastier, as Esau denounced Jacob as a class enemy, his red hair denoting both his politics and his fiery temper. The square table, off which the family dined, became their ideological boxing ring, forcing Carp to assume the unaccustomed role of referee. But he was not disinterested. After the kids had gone to bed he often confessed to his wife – Hetty – that his sympathies were with Esau, whose ideology – like his own – did not include appeasement or forgiveness. At heart he was still a boxer; an eye-for-an-eye man. In fact he still had issues with most European countries, and refused to book a continental holiday, favouring the more innocent charms of Westcliff, Cliftonville, and Bournemouth. But in 1960 Salmon took his family to the Lido di Jesolo – near Venice – and the following summer Hetty insisted that he do the same.

Relations between Carp and Salmon were as cordial as ever, maybe even more so, now that he had abandoned his father's profession, and accepted his old friend's invitation to join the furniture manufacturers he ran with his brothers, as their head of marketing. Hetty was delighted by her husband's sudden elevation into the world of white-collar employment, but (gratitude aside) remained ever vigilant for signs of condescension from Carp's employer and – more particularly – his wife.

Taking advice from the Salmons they booked rooms at the Hotel Faro, insisting (as the Salmons had done) that they were adjacent, and had balconies overlooking the long beach and the Adriatic beyond. The first evening, after a day of swimming and sun-bathing (tainted only by an excess of German speakers), the family assembled on the balcony of Room 352. Carp wandered to the edge, where the sun still shone, and leaned his elbows on the wall, which was topped off with a shelf of grey slate. Something caught his eye, and his gaze shifted from the infinite horizon to the microcosmic world beneath his nose, where – as it happened – a pocket-sized drama was being played out.

The participants attracted attention, despite their minute proportions, on account of their brilliant colouring. Carp was green-fingered, and knew a red spider mite when he saw one. But unless he was mistaken there seemed to be two sorts; one with visible legs that looked like you'd expect given their nomenclature, and another – much more numerous – that resembled nothing so much as a self-propelling pin-head.

The former, the ones that matched their name, patrolled endlessly, as if policing their own square inch of slate, while the smaller of the species scurried blindly, in constant motion to no apparent purpose. Every once in a while a couple of the spidery types paired off, and performed an aggressive pasodoble, as if they were dancers or matadors, though Carp preferred to imagine them as boxers. He summoned his sons, like some Old-Testament patriarch who'd had a vision.

"Take a look," he said, nodding towards the insects. "It seems but yesterday that our jolly neighbours on the beach were of the opinion that you, me, and your mother were vermin who deserved no better than this."

Making a fist of his mighty hand he brought it down God-like on the red spider mites, many of whom perished.

Cautiously the survivors regrouped, and instinctively reconstituted the former class structure.

"See how the masses run!" said Esau, with all the authority of a teenage autodidact. "They have unity but no leadership, a necessity if they are to overthrow the hegemony of the bigger mites and establish equality. They are not red for nothing."

"Pie-in-the-sky," said Jacob. "Leadership will come from the more enlightened of the superior bugs, or from nowhere."

"And how will they obtain the attention – not to mention the trust – of their class enemies?" said Esau.

"Why with laughter, of course," said Jacob. "Count their legs. They were born to tickle."

To him they were arachnid disciples of Harpo Marx, whose original wigs were deepest red, a fact he owed to Salmon's oldest.

As his father had done, not many minutes before, Esau raised his fist, intending to smite his brother.

"I salute your dialectical skills," said Jacob. "But before you thump me allow me to remind you of another Marxist gem. The first people to disappear when a country turns totalitarian, noted Groucho, are its comics and its comedians. The rest is not silence, but insanity."

Esau remained unpersuaded. But his mother intervened, before that second blow could be struck.

"Enough already with the philosophical discourse," she said. "Has it not occurred to either of you geniuses that the variation in size might simply be due to different stages of development. In which case the smaller mites are – how do you call them – larvae? And like youth everywhere they have energy in excess. It's their parents I pity."

"You are all ..." said Esau, straining for an insult commensurate with his anger, " ... you are all Mensheviks!"

For his holiday reading Esau had plucked Trotsky's *History of the Russian Revolution* from his father's bookshelves, while Jacob had packed *The Tales of Hoffmann*.

"You know," he said, when they were both reading in bed, "I do hope the story they tell about our surname is true. I rather like having my origins in the imagination of a writer like Hoffmann. Actually there are times when I feel I may be a character in one of his stories."

"How typical," said Esau, "how handy to be able to blame someone else for your moral failings."

****

On the morning of the family's first visit to Venice, Esau refused to get out of bed citing ideological objections.

"Why would I want to visit the St Petersburg of the south?" he said.

"Because if you won't none of us will," said his mother, "we can't leave you here alone."

"Too bad," said Esau, "the class struggle requires sacrifice."

"Communism represents the will of the masses, don't you agree?" said his twin.

"Naturally," said Esau.

"Well there are three of us and only one of you," said Jacob.

"The bourgeoisie are not the masses," said Esau, placing a pillow over his head.

At which point Carp intervened.

"Name me one Venetian Jew," he said.

"Shylock of course," said Esau.

"My son the antisemite," said Carp. "Try Daniele Manin instead. Leader of the glorious 1848 revolt against the island's Hapsburg occupiers. Okay, it wasn't the siege of Leningrad, but for 500 days Manin and his followers held the Austrians at bay. The first thing we'll do on arrival in Venice is pay homage at his tomb. Word of honour."

Thus was Esau persuaded to ride with the others on the bus to Punta Sabbioni, from where they caught the ferry to Venice. Even stubborn Esau was staggered – or perhaps it was the motion of the boat – by the sight of its red towers, latticed palaces, and domed churches, all apparently floating on a gilded meniscus in defiance of that universal nemesis – gravity. It was, in other words, the locus of humanity's rebellion against the iron laws of nature.

Manin's more modest revolution was finally crushed in 1849, and its exiled leader lived out the remainder of his days teaching conversational Italian to Parisians. Twelve years after his death in 1857 he was repatriated. Thousands lined the Grand Canal to cheer as the gondola bearing his remains passed by. Nevertheless, he was denied burial in St Mark's Basilica on account of his Jewish ancestry. Instead he was laid to rest to the left of the Basilica in Piazzetta dei Leoncini, his sarcophagus guarded by a pair of stone lions. Esau patted the one, Jacob the other. Carp intoned the mourner's Kaddish for a fellow fighter.

****

While their parents were haggling over the price of some glass beads with matching earrings in Giurovich's jewellery store near St Mark's Square, the twins – in concert for once – decided to explore the neighbouring alleys on their own. Without a word to their parents, without any forethought, they crossed first one bridge, then another, and then a third, progressing (though they did not know it) in a zig-zag fashion along the Rio Della Fava, until they caught sight of a landmark they recognized – the Rialto – which they thought was very near their starting point, to which they resolved to return.

Of course they argued over which way to progress from the bridge, tossed a 500 lira coin, and Esau – who correctly called heads – got to pick. Unfortunately he elected to go north rather than south. Thus the twins continued in the wrong direction, unconsciously gravitating towards the Campo del Ghetto. When they emerged into the square walled in by the tallest tenements in Venice, even Esau had to agree as his brother exclaimed: "One thing's for sure. St Mark's Square this ain't."

Not far from them was a youth in his late teens. The foreshadow of a mustache indicated that he was likely older than them. But he was wearing tortoise-shell glasses, and looked friendly enough. A state-of-the-art Olympus hung from his neck like a pectoral cross. And he was holding something they needed: a map. As soon as they introduced themselves he smiled, and held out his hand for first Esau then Jacob to shake. This was a novelty; all previous encounters with strangers had been conducted through their parents.

"Are you on holiday?" said Jacob.

"No," said Yusef, "I am in Venice to find myself."

"It seems we have achieved exactly the opposite," said Jacob.

Yusef looked at the twins; the one with red hair, and the other with black curls, but both with noses as beaky as his own.

"Perhaps you thought I am Italian," he said. "But I am – like the Wise Men – from the East. You know where is Jordan? Well, we have a nice house in its capital. My father is an officer in the Arab Legion. He was trained by Abu Hunaik, your Glubb Pasha. Even so we are not Jordanian. Both my parents come from Palestine. You have heard of Palestine?"

Esau and Jacob nodded, even though they knew it by another name.

"Perhaps then you know of Lydda? Or perhaps not: now that it's called Lod. But I am speaking of a time when it was still known as Lydda. My parents met and married there. They created a home there. Their first child was born there. All before the creation of Israel, before the Nakba, as we call it. In 1948 the Israelis – led by Moshe Dayan – took our town. They broke into our house and pointed to me – I was five – and to my mother and said to her: He can stay, you can stay. Then they pointed to my father and said: But he has to go."

"Why?" said Esau. "Why could your mother remain, but not your father?"

"That question bothered me too" said Yusef, "and for years I had no idea what the answer could be. But about three months ago my little brother came home from school and said: 'Mama is it true you are Ashkenazi?' Of course he had no idea what an Ashkenazi was, any more than I did. But our mother went crazy – like a madwoman. We had to be sent away to our room until she had regained control of herself. Only then did she allow our father to tell us that our mother's family – many hundreds of years ago – once inhabited this place – this Ghetto. How could that be? My mother was more fierce than the fiercest of the fedayeen. Whenever they spilled Israeli blood was a holiday for her. She was, it is now clear, her own worst enemy. You see, my friends, there are more scary things than getting lost. You might not know where you are, but I am in bigger trouble: I do not know who I am. I am like a land divided, unsure which side I am on. Either way, half of me is the enemy."

"We are no different," said Esau, "except that we are not in the same body."

The sun was sinking; shadows were creeping along the Campo like bars. Yusef unfolded the map, and together they plotted a route back to St Mark's Square.

"I hope you find your way," said Yusef.

"And we hope you find yourself," said the boys.

Not knowing what else to do Carp and Hetty waited beside Manin's tomb for the twins. When they reappeared, long after darkness had fallen, Carp raised his hands to the boys for the first time in his life, slapping both on their exposed cheeks, one forehand, the other backhand. Neither boy cried. That they left to their parents.

****

Esau felt the injustice of the blow far more deeply than Jacob, who recognized it for what it was: a palpable expression of love, albeit one that left red welts instead of the crimson skid marks of a stolen kiss. By the time the ferry docked at Punta Sabbioni, the slaps were history, and their visible traces no more, at least as far as Jacob was concerned. But Esau refused to forget, and nurtured their memory within, where they festered. Even while they were still at Jesolo he provoked arguments with his father, probing for his more sensitive spots, the most sensitive of which – he quickly realized – concerned the Jewish homeland itself.

On the beach Carp sighed as though the chorus of German glee – a combination of parents and children playing ball, or splashing in the surf – were a not-so-distant echo of the Nuremberg rallies, and ostentatiously covered his ears with his hands.

"You can block your ears all you want," said Esau, "but it won't hide the truth that today's most diligent disciples of the Nazis are your Zionists."

Carp leapt from his deck-chair, as if he had sat on a jelly fish. His body, coated in Ambre Solaire, gleamed like a Greek statue. Anyone could see that boxer shorts were not named boxer shorts for no reason. In case there was still any doubt Carp raised his fists.

"Stand up and take your punishment like a man," he said.

Esau retained his reclining position and laughed, enraging his father the more, and causing him to snort like a wild beast.

"Have you gone potty?" said Hetty, also rising. "Are you

really prepared to beat your own son in front of the Boche? Tell me, what will they think of us? That their Führer was right? That Jews are no better than animals? Is that what you want? To hand another victory to Hitler?"

The confrontation ended unresolved when Esau chose to leave the beach. But he seemed unable to cease his invective, and the goading of his father. He scoffed at the insults suffered by the local hero, Daniele Manin, and insisted they were nothing compared to the vicissitudes endured by Yusef and his family, at the hands of Carp's great hero – Moshe Dayan – no less.

"As Nelson held the telescope to his blind eye and said, 'What signals?'" he hissed across the table in the hotel restaurant, "so Moshe Dayan observes the Palestinians with his dead eye and asks, 'What injustices?'"

Only Hetty's fearsome glare prevented Carp from tossing his plate of spaghetti at his son. Esau no longer referred to Israel's War of Independence, but to the Nakba.

****

University provided some respite, but a great schism was inevitable. It arrived in 1967, a minor consequence of the Six Day War. At that time Esau was researching his doctorate at SOAS, while Jacob was doing the same at UEA. Different cities, different disciplines: London vs Norwich; International Law vs Literature. In the one Esau sought to criminalize Israel's founding fathers; whereas Jacob was dead set on rehabilitating Shylock, Fagin, Svengali et al.

Worried that he was a witness to the destruction of Israel, Jacob journeyed down to Rex House in London, and volunteered to help on the home front. But by the time he flew out – in mid-July – the war was long-since won. Esau ridiculed such fears, and mocked his brother's second-hand heroics. As far as he was concerned the war was an imperialist plot, a trap into which Nasser and his allies had fallen. Israel's conquests – miraculous accidents to many – were to him all part of a master plan to confiscate and colonize vast dunams of Jordan, Syria, and Egypt.

On hearing those arguments Carp said, "That boy would buy the Protocols," and banned him from the family home. "What do young people say these days?" he said to Hetty. "The political has become personal. Well, it has in our family."

****

Never an anti-Zionist like his brother, Jacob nonetheless grew increasingly critical of Israel's governing classes, more urgently after the assassination of Yitzhak Rabin, and the rise of Bobo Sobol, whom he despised above all other Israelis. While at Norwich he had founded a satirical magazine called *Meshuga*, which he continued to publish occasionally under the imprint of the Red Spider Mite Press, even after he had acquired a wife, a family, and academic tenure. Early in 2012 he ran an editorial dedicated to the worries that beset a Prime Minister, especially an Israeli one:

"Bobo has insomnia. Perhaps for the first time in his life. Does not even lay head to pillow. What troubles him so? The moral collapse of the country he leads as Prime Minister? The fact that Israel – once so admired – is now bested only by North Korea as the most loathed society on the globe? In your dreams! What is keeping Bobo awake is not the state of the nation, but the state of his hair. Yesterday his combover was an insurance policy; today it has become a necessity. He knows – with the absolute certainty of an ideologue – that were he even to take a nap he would awaken exposed as a bald man. And he knows too – with equal certainty – that Rebekah – on seeing him as such – would bring down the walls with hysterical screams, which she would explain by saying that she had mistaken him for a pig. But Bobo is a cunning man. A man to whom truth is not only a stranger, but an actual enemy. Inspired he rises from the marital bed and enters the en suite. Quickly he finds what he is looking for, and facing the mirror, crowns himself King of Israel with one of Rebekah's hair nets.

"Even so, the situation remains dangerously dynamic, hair loss being a continuing process, and – for him – a threat as big as terrorism. Inevitably, the area that needs to be covered increases, so that Bobo's parting comes to resemble his country's unstable eastern border. Thus the Prime Minister becomes an advertisement for his own policies; all show and no substance. Worse, the Israel he has created has become a land without foundation, an illusion that cannot be sustained *m'dor l'dor*, from generation to generation. Can the country yet escape from the curse of Rebekah's hair net, or is it already too late? Only God knows. So let Him send a mighty wind that will expose the combover for what it is, and reveal what it covers up – *nada*, *efes*, nothing."

"You still don't get it," wrote Esau, upon receipt of the magazine. "Bobo is no false prophet. He is Mr Israel."

****

In the Spring of that year – 2012 – the Globe Theatre organized a Cultural Olympiad called Globe to Globe – during which all of Shakespeare's 37 plays were to be staged by as many foreign companies, all performing in their native tongue. Since Carp's 92nd birthday fell on the same day as the Habima Theatre's production of *The Merchant of Venice*, Jacob booked him a ticket as a present. Because his father had been a widower for some time, he got himself a ticket too. As a matter of fact, Hetty had died of heart failure a decade earlier, but Carp retained the figure and vitality – if not quite the punch – of the feather-weight champion he had once been. He still lived in the same semi-detached in which he and Hetty had raised their sons, though he had hardly seen Esau since the funeral. Jacob, on the contrary, remained dutiful and more.

A few days ahead of the performance he had received a letter from the Globe advising all ticket-holders to arrive well before the start on account of the extra security required that night. So he picked up his father at five, and they joined the queue to enter the theatre an hour later. Opposite the audience-in-waiting, as it conga-danced along the pavement, was a bunch of Englishmen with doleful countenances, whose banners identified them as Christian lovers of Zion. Further away – behind a police cordon – were a score or more of sterner-looking citizens bunched under Palestinian flags. At their head was some Marianne who tunelessly sang songs of freedom.

"Do you think our Esau is among them?" said Carp. "You know he signed the letter in *The Guardian* demanding that the Globe withdraw its invitation to the Habima?"

"What else is new?" said Jacob.

"This should have been a great day for us," said his father. "A Jewish company has been invited to perform one of Shakespeare's plays – and not any play – in the language of the State of Israel. And not just at any venue, either. But what happens? I'll tell you what happens: a bunch of momzers decides to spoil our big day. It's not enough for them that they boycott the production; no, they want it cancelled altogether. For why? On account of a new blood libel, that's for why. I'm not a fool, I know that blood was spilled back in '48. But the way I see it is this: the Israelis and the Arabs were like two heavyweights. It was a terrible fight, no one is denying that. But one side was the unanimous winner, a verdict the Arabs refused to accept. Instead they have forced rematch after rematch, losing so many times they have stolen the world's sympathy. Perhaps we should throw the next fight, and bask in universal understanding while the Arabs cut our throats."

****

How differently the Habima was treated from all the other companies only became fully apparent when they entered the theatre, which had been transformed for the night into an international airport, complete with uniformed police, beefed-up security officials, bag searches, sniffer dogs, and full-body scans.

"It is a curious turn of events," said Jacob, while some sort of beagle was giving his private parts the all-clear, "when Jews line up to see an antisemitic play, and antisemites do their best to stop them."

Eventually the audience was accommodated, some in seats, others amid the groundlings, and the actors of the Habima began to recite the dialogue, not in the language of Shakespeare, but of Shylock. It shamed Jacob that his father could follow it much better than he. Even so he was attuned to the universal frisson when it came time for Shylock to deliver his great speech.

At first the audience sat in silent wonderment as this despised and finally broken man declaimed: "Hath not a Jew hands, organs, dimensions, senses, affections, passions?"

As the rhythmic words rolled on a blackbird alighted at the very summit of the Globe's gable and – opening his bill – began to accompany Shylock, contrasting unfettered joy with the burdens humans pile one upon the other. " ... If you prick us," continued Shylock, "do we not bleed? If you tickle us, do we not laugh?"

At which point a third voice was heard from among the groundlings: "Palestinians are human beans too! If you shoot them, do they not die?"

Or something like that. It belonged, of course, to Esau. Muscular men, employed for the night, removed him, though not before he bowed his head – topped still with fiery curls – in the direction of his father.

Other interruptions followed at intervals – "Shame on you Habima!", "Jews out of Palestine" – and each time the protester was seamlessly evicted.

"You know what," said Jacob, during the interval, "rather than create a disruption, these small disturbances actually add another layer to the theatrical experience. They don't call Shakespeare our contemporary for nothing."

As it happened he probably sympathized with many of the protestors' views. Just because you are an antisemite, he liked to say, doesn't make you wrong a priori.

"That last one was lucky I didn't get my hands on him," said Carp. "What do those bastards want of us? First they tell us to go back to Palestine, now they want us out of it."

"I remember a conversation I had years ago with your friend, David Salmon," said Jacob, "probably around the time Dustin Hoffman was in town playing Shylock at the Phoenix.

I asked him if he fancied seeing it with me. But he declined, offering the opinion that the only Hollywood actor worthy of the role was Groucho Marx."

"Personally I'd have cast John Garfield," said his father, "and found him a good lawyer."

"Maybe," said Jacob. "But Groucho? That really would have been an eye-opener."

****

After the intermission Shylock almost got his pound of flesh, but didn't quite, thanks to Portia, and was last seen skulking off the stage with a suitcase. As the theatre emptied onto New Globe Walk, Jacob noticed that the entire audience was being filmed by a black-bearded mullah wearing a white tunic – called a tarim shirt, Jacob later learned – and a kufi. It felt like a threatening act to Jacob, so he approached a policeman and complained.

The officer replied: "Well, sir, may I suggest that if you don't want to be photographed by the gentleman, you move away from him."

But that is just what Jacob could not do. One look at the fuming cinematographer – a Mad Mullah out of central casting – was enough to show him that tickling would never make him laugh. The only alternative was to make others laugh at him.

****

Obviously an emergency issue of his occasional magazine was called for. Its cover came easily. Recalling that *Time* annually displayed a Man (or Woman) of the year on its cover, Jacob decided to elect a Meshuggener of the Month, the only candidate being the Mad Mullah of the Globe. He commissioned his regular cartoonist to produce a mug shot, based upon his own eye-witness description. For once the cartoonist chose to work anonymously, after his wife reminded him that Kurt Westergaard – the Dane who drew the cartoon of Muhammad with a bomb in his turban – had recently attracted the attention of an axe-wielding meshuggener from Al Shabab.

"If he were Dracula I could instruct you how to protect yourself," said Jacob. "But a jihadist? That's a tough one."

"Westergaard had a panic room," said the cartoonist, "I don't."

"Maybe a pork chop would stop him in his tracks, as garlic does a vampire," said Jacob. "As well as being *haraam*, it could be mistaken for a pistol. If that doesn't succeed, try reading from Salman Rushdie's *Satanic Verses*. That should scare him off. But if it doesn't you've still got the nuclear option: a portrait of the Prophet himself. Should all three fail to deter him you can rest assured that your jihadist is an imposter."

The cartoonist elected to remain uncredited.

Jacob had no such inhibitions. Research into Muhammed's sense of humour revealed that he had been known to smile, though there was some dispute as to whether he had ever actually laughed. It was not something he advised: "Do not laugh too much, for laughing too much deadens the heart." Jokes were permitted, however, providing eleven prohibitions were observed. Jacob dedicated the emergency issue of *Meshuga* to trashing every one.

In the editorial, in which he discussed events at the Globe, he imagined some jihadi fanatic scrutinizing the footage in slo-mo while noting down the names of those he recognized among the departing audience. It didn't matter if they were prominent or obscure; he was an equal-opportunity assassin. Among the many Jacob had noted were the Chief Rabbi, and – sitting on the opposite side of the theatre – the rabbi from his own synagogue, who – before the summer was out – would be intoning the prayers at his funeral.

****

Esau had been called upon to identify the body. Afterwards he was unable to remove the image from his mind, or the thought that his brother – his only brother, whom he loved despite everything – had been brought down by a plague of red spider mites. Esau counted six bullet holes on Jacob's white shirt, each with its own leggy areola. He remembered the words he had called out from the pit that night at the Globe. He remembered also that late afternoon on the balcony of the Hotel Faro when he had bunched his fists and would have beaten his twin if their mother had not intervened. Guilt overwhelmed him as if it were something animate. He could feel it compressing his lungs, and he wrestled with the physical sensation, as his brother's namesake had wrestled with the angel at Jabbok. Why? Because he felt complicit in the crime, as if his action in Jesolo had initiated a chain of events that led inevitably to Jacob's assassination. Was he worse than an Esau, was he a Cain?

He resolved to disconnect from his erstwhile associates; if not from the struggle for Palestine itself, then from his fellow strugglers, whose world-view was making him feel increasingly uncomfortable. Of course that did not include Yusef. Remember Yusef?

Twenty years ago, a mature student had knocked on Esau's office door at SOAS – where he taught Political Science – and asked if he could be persuaded to supervise his doctoral thesis, provisionally entitled: Palestine: A State of Mind. Only when Yusef recounted his family history, many weeks later, did Esau exclaim: "There cannot be two with such a past. Unless you have a brother."

"No brother," said Yusef.

"Well, I have one," said Esau, "a twin. Perhaps you remember us as two lost boys, trying to find their way out of the Ghetto in Venice. You were our guide."

"Now you have the opportunity of returning the favour," said Yusef.

Yusef habitually turned up for the tutorials in bespoke Islamic outfits, which prompted Esau to conclude his revelation with the words: "It seems that you have found yourself then."

"If a man does not know who he is as he approaches three score and ten," said Yusef, "then he has lived in vain."

His march to self-knowledge had been a long one. First there had been the issue of his dual identity, which he had finally resolved, only to be confronted with the secular vs religion controversy. In the early years his sympathies had been wholeheartedly with the secularists. His Master's dissertation on the unique purity of George Habash's PFLP was testimony to that. But the word "purity", so prominently placed, was a clue to how things would change.

Yusef was honest enough to admit that the toppling of the Twin Towers had occasioned a major shift in his own tectonic plates.

"Every atom of my intellect had been repulsed by that murderous act," he said, "but the truth was that at some deeper level I found it empowering. Almost without my noticing I began making more and more public appearances in traditional dress."

He paused, as if to give time for Esau to respond. But Esau said nothing.

"Like it or not," continued Yusef, "the act was biblical in its terrible beauty. Like when Samson felled the temple of Dagon."

Then he asked after Jacob.

In those days Professor Carp was still teaching English & American Literature at the University of East Anglia, and was the author of two successful critical studies: *Shylock's Revenge: How the Villain Became the Hero*, and *I Put a Spell on You: Jews in the Works of Du Maurier, Rider Haggard and Le Carré.*

By the time the Habima came to the Globe both Esau and Yusef were in the forefront of the anti-Zionist BDS campaign, and regarded themselves as comrades-in-arms.

****

Jacob's funeral was held at the crematorium in Golders Green. Since his killer was still at large – and likely a terrorist – the chapel was guarded by armed police, some with automatic weapons at the ready. The mourners were frisked according to gender. It was, all agreed, an unlikely end for an academic.

Jacob's wife and three daughters – two with husbands – occupied the front row. Esau and his father slipped into the row behind. His partner had refused to attend on account of Jacob's politics, a decision that caused Esau to reconsider the relationship. During the eulogies Carp would not be silenced;

he knew his son, and didn't need any third party to elaborate his virtues.

"In every generation there are a bunch of momzers who want to do away with us," he said to his surviving son. "In your grandfather's time it was the Russians; in mine it was the Nazis; and in yours it's the Muslims. Tell me, Esau, what has the world got against us? Are we really so wicked?"

Esau considered a range of sociopolitical answers, but knew that none of them would satisfy his father. And why should they? This was not political science, it was personal. He looked at the back of his sister-in-law, upon which was made visible the passage of grief through her body. Its progress shook her mercilessly, making it seem that she were having some sort of convulsion or fit. That was the moment when Esau decided to put an end to his relationship. It was a decision made rationally, but what happened next he could neither control nor explain. He turned towards his father and hugged the old man, weeping as he did so. Old Carp in response rested his head on his son's shoulder, and loudly lamented his loss. There they stood, holding one another like two veteran boxers who had fought one another to the point of exhaustion, while Jacob's body slid slowly into the furnace, and – from out of nowhere – Groucho Marx (as Captain Spaulding, the African Explorer) sang:

"Hello, I must be going,
I cannot stay, I came to say, I must be going.
I'm glad I came, but just the same I must be going."

As the congregation emptied into the car park and onto the road, Esau was surprised to see among the tombstones on the far side of Hoop Lane, a single man who seemed to have no other purpose but to film the mourners. His first assumption was that he was a member of the team assigned to protect them. But then he had second thoughts. For the man behind the camera looked a lot like his good friend Yusef.

Shylock Our Contemporary

"ADMIT IT," I say to my father, "we are lost. How many more times do we have to cross the Rialto to convince you?"

My father drops the handle of the case he has been wheeling, passes me the iPhone and says: "Okay, Marco Polo, you do better."

Accepting the gender reversal without comment, I linger in *pays inconnu* waiting for Google Maps to rediscover us. As if springing from that empty pocket of existence a man in a long black gaberdine suddenly appears, only to jostle me aside. The coat is noteworthy, for the day is scorching, and the wearer is not an orthodox Jew. But he is certainly in a hurry. Having pushed past me he leaps upon the bridge's parapet, as if goaded beyond endurance by the soft-shoe shuffle of the impenetrable crowd, and begins to exercise his freedom to run. Having reached the summit he pauses, and spreads his arms, like the star of a musical about to deliver his climactic number. But instead of some rousing chorus he issues a filthy imprecation, and leaps feet first into the turbulent waters of the Grand Canal.

By some miracle he is not crushed by itinerant water buses, vaporettos, or even the local *traghetto*, but that seems to be about the extent of his good fortune. For example, it soon becomes evident that the man cannot swim. Nor are the numerous spectators over-sympathetic to his plight. Some film his struggles with their mobiles, laughing all the while. Others point south and yell: "Africa is that way!" Moves to assist him are the exception. Three lifebelts are tossed towards his head like quoits. All miss their intended target, but splash down near enough, making it seem strange that the man does not try to reach them. Perhaps he wants to drown. But that is no excuse to let him. Are all of the spectators so stone-hearted that not one is prepared to jump in and rescue him? I do not exempt myself. After all, did I not recently earn my bronze medal in life saving? True, I trained in the school swimming pool. But water is water. I had better make up my mind. Soon such questions will be academic. The drowning man's coat has spread wide, and continues to buoy him up, giving him the opportunity to chant something that sounds like the snatches of some long-remembered tune, or is maybe a tribal death chant. But the garment is more or less saturated, and is beginning to drag the poor wretch down to muddy death.

At which point my father suddenly says: "I can't take any more of this!"

Then he slips off his jacket and his Blundstones, says, "Keep an eye on these," and leaps into the canal, apparently indifferent to the perils of passing traffic and the harmful bacteria lurking in every mouthful of its toxic waters. My father is not a graceful swimmer; he progresses slowly like a gargantuan toad. To complicate matters the man, ingratitude personified, refuses to accept his saviour with open arms, but my father persists, and finally drags the reluctant pedestrian onto terra firma, assisted in the end by two idle gondoliers.

My father is still dripping when – guided by an admiring *polizia locale*, and pursued by a few regional pressmen – we finally reach our obscure hotel. Venice is small, and word travels fast within it. Professor Shaul Bassi is already awaiting us with towels. Moreover, he has brought a doctor from his university to administer shots against hepatitis, jaundice, tetanus, diphtheria, and God knows what else.

"I can see the headline already," says Professor Bassi, as the hacks continue to question my father, "Shylock saves Othello."

It is five hundred years since the founding of the world's first ghetto, right here in Venice, and the Professor is the co-ordinator of the quincentennial commemorations, which culminate this week, with a five-night-only production of *The Merchant of Venice* on its villain's home turf. Hence his reference to Shylock, the man of the moment. Hence, also, our presence; my father being one of the sine qua nons of Shakespearean scholarship.

Turning in my direction Professor Bassi says: "Tell me, Jessica, what does it feel like to be the daughter of a man who is a hero to half of Venice? Needless to say, the other half thinks he should have let the shvartzer drown."

I blush and reply that I am very proud of him. But, to tell you the truth, like Venice, I am in two minds: in saving the drowning man my father had put his own life at risk, a risk of some moment, since I do not have a spare parent.

****

My mother ended her days in a cancer ward six years ago, when I was a prepubescent thirteen. The doctor who ran the ward wore a gold crucifix around her neck. I remember my father once saying to her: "How can you come to such a place every day and still believe in God?" To which she replied: "You have it the wrong way round. It is because I believe in Him that I come every day."

My father collected me from school every afternoon and drove us to visit my mother, except on Thursdays when I had saxophone lessons with Robin de Smet, who was as far removed from James Brown as it is possible to be (his ancestors did not toil in the fields, but painted them, being Belgian impressionists). Nevertheless, he agreed to help me learn "I Feel Good", which I had volunteered to play at my school's summer concert. Neither parent was among the audience: my mother too sick, of course; my father too wedded to her bedside.

"How did it go?" said my father, when he picked me up afterwards.

"A standing ovation," I said immodestly.

"There was an incident in the hospital," said my father. "Something uncanny. About 8.30 your mother suddenly sat bolt upright, and began to move her arms, as if in response to some inaudible sound. A nurse rushed over, but I held up my hand. For now I too could hear the sound. It was your mother humming, 'I Feel Good'."

Not long afterwards I overheard a doctor, the one in charge of pain-relief, whisper to my father that he had never before treated someone with such intractable pain, and that however much diamorphine he administered it was never enough. In the end they gave her such large doses that she was permanently comatose.

On practically every visit to the ward someone else died, and the curtains were hurriedly drawn around their bed. I knew it was only a matter of days before it would be my mother's turn. Dry-eyed I began to imagine that she was already dead, and with that came the dread that I would not cry when it really happened. I mentioned this fear to my father who said: "'What's Hecuba to him or he to Hecuba/ That he should weep for her?' It is not a requirement to show feelings to prove that you really have them."

But that wasn't my point. I didn't care what others thought. My concern was that I wouldn't have the feelings. As a matter of fact, I did cry when she died. I think it was the sight of my father trying to remove the wedding ring from her dead hand that unhinged me.

****

In the years that followed my father proved to be a permissive parent, except for one non-negotiable rule, which he called the Prime Directive: I must never-ever use my mother's early death as an excuse for bad behaviour.

When I was sixteen my father published the book that made his name, that turned him from an obscure lecturer in Shakespearean Studies at the University of St Albans, into a full professor, and an habitué of international conferences. Whenever possible my father took me with him. I am not yet twenty, and already have been feted in (to name a few): Los Angeles, Lima, Stockholm, Madrid, Prague, Paris, and Jerusalem. Why should I behave badly?

My father called his book: *Shylock Our Contemporary.* Among others it drew him to the attention of Shaul Bassi, who has invited him to deliver a keynote address at the Doge's Palace, scene of the infamous "pound of flesh" trial, where, by way of atonement, the Doge's successors have mounted an exhibition entitled, "Venice, the Jews, and Europe 1516-2016".

We visit it on the following afternoon – even we can find our own way to the Doge's Palace – just the two of us, father and daughter.

"What do you think of it?" I say, as we wander around the palatial halls.

"If you want a crash course in Ghettology," says my father, "this is the place to be."

Shylock – impersonated by Sir Laurence Olivier, no less – is an inevitable presence, of course. Flickering on a screen – like some shade in Hades – he is condemned to endlessly repeat his most famous speech.

My father quotes it too, later that evening, during the course of his lecture, when he gives equal weight to its lesson in civics and shared humanity – "Hath not a Jew eyes etc," – and to its furious conclusion – "The villainy you/ teach me, I will execute, and it shall go hard but I/ will better the instruction." He concludes, controversially, that in those pulsating lines Shakespeare had prophesied the conflicting policies that were tearing Israel apart, and that it was the vengeful Jew who was emerging triumphant.

After the lecture, when questions are encouraged, someone demands: "Name a contemporary Shylock!"

"Easy," says my father, "Sheldon Adelson, owner of the Venetian in Las Vegas."

"Too pat," says someone else, "give us another name."

"Sure," says my father, "Donald Trump."

"How can that be?" says the questioner. "He isn't even Jewish."

"Maybe not, but I'll wager my house that most of you here think of him as Antonio thought of Shylock. Okay, I know it's almost de rigeur these days to present the latter as humanity's ambassador in Venice – or, if you prefer, the goody. In this post-Holocaust age of ours it's the honourable thing to do. But alas for the elevation of Shylock, the play has a fifth act, in which he is all but forgotten in the rush for reconciliation at Belmont. Accepting Shylock as the baddie does allow us to better see Shylock as Shakespeare saw him. For him the Doge's verdict, especially the forced conversion – which is wholly abhorrent to us – could well have represented an act of redemption, Shylock's key to heaven. Fortunately Hillary Clinton – surely Portia to Trump's Shylock – seems to already have her hands on the keys to the White House. But if – God forbid – Trump were to win there will be plenty to cheer him on as he trashes Belmont. Some might even see it as the revenge of the deplorables, among whose number stands Shylock."

Over dinner Professor Bassi calls the lecture a triumph, but my father seems strangely moody, as though he had eaten something sour. It is already late when we set off for our tiny hotel – more like a *pensione* – in its tiny street.

When my mother was alive she did the navigating, while my father did the driving. Perhaps he became too dependent upon her map-reading skills, but without her he is lost. We are both lost, in fact, for I have inherited my father's non-existent sense of direction. The chimes of midnight ring, and still we are wandering the streets of Venice, *sans* map, *sans* signal, *sans* hope. After ninety minutes of increasingly desperate exploration we emerge from an alley into a deserted Campo with at least five exits.

"You know what," I say "why don't we check our phones? Maybe there'll be a signal here."

"You do what you like," says my father, "but I'll go crazy if I stand still."

"Just for a minute longer," I say.

Within moments the phone has calculated a route to our destination, which turns out to be a mere three minutes away. I raise my head in triumph, only to discover that I am quite alone in an empty square. What to do? I have no idea which of the five exits my father has taken. Do I stay or do I go? At the exact moment I decide to desert my father he reappears.

****

The next day is Shaul Bassi's big day; Shylock's too. On how many other days is his Appeal against the Doge's harsh sentence heard by an Associate Justice of the Supreme Court of the United States?

After lunch Professor Bassi says: "I've got to check that all the Judges are happy. Are you sure you can find your way to the Scuola Grande di San Rocco without me?"

"Don't worry," I say, "I've already mapped out the route."

But once we are alone my father announces that he needs to go back to the hotel.

"Are you crazy?" I say. "You know what will happen."

"Just look at me," he says, "I am sweating like a pig, and very probably smell like one too. No way am I going to appear looking like this in front of Jim and Stephen."

He means Professors Shapiro and Greenblat, along with my father the Supremes of Shakespeare studies. This performance is entirely out of character. Never before have I heard my father express concern about his appearance. No matter, he is in earnest now. As predicted, we are unable to find the hotel. After an hour of strenuous but misguided walking my father's face is the colour of a red stop-light, and his shirt is sticking to his back.

"Look," I say, pointing to the wall of a mid-size palace,

"there's a sign directing us to where we need to go. And I mean a 'sign'. If we don't take notice we'll likely miss the Appeal. Is that what you want?"

"What I want," he says, "is to find the hotel, and change into some dry clothes. Then catch the Appeal."

"But time is running out," I say. "You can't do both."

"So I'll do one," he says.

"But it's the wrong one," I say.

"Do what you like," he says, "I have no choice."

To my amazement I do. As we part I can't help wondering if I'll ever set eyes on my father again. Just as I am about to abandon hope he suddenly appears trotting in the direction of the Scuola Grande di San Rocco, looking outrageously smart in a midnight blue linen suit with matching tie, items of clothing I do not recall having seen before.

"I'm impressed that you found your way back to the hotel, changed, then hot-footed it here in record time," I say.

"Don't be," he says, "I cheated. I saw this stuff in a shop window. So I went in, made sure it all fitted, and bought the lot."

After all the hysteria we take our seats with several minutes to spare.

"My God," says my father, "this place has been well chosen. Shylock may be our contemporary, but this place is Shakespeare's. And just look at all the Tintorettos. The canvases up here in the Chapter Room were completed in 1581, making them of an age – give or take a decade – with *The Merchant of Venice*. And have you noticed that all the paintings on the ceiling relate to the Old Testament? The big ones depict scenes from the journey of the Israelites to the Promised Land, something we can relate to ..."

So saying he gives my hand an apologetic squeeze.

My father goes on, but my attention is distracted by one of the smaller panels above my head. It depicts in kinetic detail the Akedah, or the Binding of Isaac. White of hair and beard old Abraham stands centre stage, his arms outstretched, as if posing for a version of the crucifixion. Except that his left hand rests upon the shoulder of his naked son, downcast upon the sacrificial pyre, and his right clutches a murderous blade. The latter is primed to deliver the fatal blow, only to be disarmed at the last by the gentle touch of an angel.

"You could call her Portia *avant la lettre*," says my father, as if reading my mind.

The ceiling may belong to the Old Testament, but the walls of the Chapter Room are the province of the New, featuring episodes from the life of Christ. Naturally my father sees this as more than coincidental.

"Amazing," he says, "the Chapter Room itself illustrates the Merchant's essential conflict; between the religion of the Son, and the religion of the Father. One of whose major points of friction is, of course, that between mercy – a quality in which Shylock, as a Jew, is supposedly deficient – and justice. You remember how the Doge greets Antonio at the beginning of the trial? 'I am sorry for thee: thou art come to answer/ A stony adversary, an inhuman wretch/ uncapable of pity, void and empty/From any dram of mercy'. Obviously today's audience – it feels more like a congregation to me – has come to witness a less partial consideration."

It feels like a congregation to me too. When the Justices enter at 5.00 pm, and we are all instructed to rise I cannot help but remember those ancient days when I accompanied my grandmother to Raleigh Close Synagogue on Yom Kippur (always sweltering in my memory) and we sat in the gallery with the other women, but rose with the men when the rabbi lifted the holy scrolls from the Ark and paraded them down the aisles. The Jurists who march down the aisle of the Chapter Room command similar respect. First among them is the Honourable (and diminutive) Ruth Bader Ginsburg, the Supreme Court Justice. She is followed by four others, also in black gowns. They take their seats before a structure that looks strangely like the Ark of the Covenant.

A Florentine represents Shylock. He tellingly compares the Alien Statute (Portia's invention, he concludes, having found no evidence for its existence outside the play) – under which Shylock is sentenced to death for threatening the life of a native Venetian, then paupered – to Mussolini's Racial Laws, which deprived Shylock's co-religionists of their rights, jobs, assets and lives.

Antonio's spokesman will have none of this: "My first comment is that it would not be appropriate to approach the matter with our contemporary sensibility, schooled by history to the atrocious outcome of anti-Jewish prejudice and persecution in the 20th century." Instead he proposes sticking to Venetian law circa 1570. Another of Antonio's defenders points out that the Appelant – that's Shylock – attended the trial with murder in mind.

"Why else," he asks, "whet his knife so earnestly?"

Good question. When all is said and done, I feel that Shylock will be lucky to win the Appeal.

While the judges retire to deliberate, the platform is given over to my father's great rivals, James Shapiro and Stephen Greenblatt, who have twenty minutes in which to turn the spotlight from law to literature, from the court to the theatre. One – maybe Shapiro – asks us to consider Portia's motives once she has heard Bassanio – her new husband – declare that he would gladly sacrifice his life and that of his wife to save Antonio. Should she then abet Antonio's murder, thereby rubbing out a rival, but also running the risk of poisoning her marriage with the gruesome memory of his martyrdom, or should she rescue him, with the attendant danger of his continuing presence? Another – I forget which – recalls a production by the Cameri Theatre of Tel Aviv, which was in rehearsal when Baruch Goldstein massacred nearly three dozen Muslims at prayer in Hebron, an act which prompted the recasting of Shylock as a West Bank settler who, becoming radicalized, turns both rabbinic and rabid.

"What have I been telling you?" says my father, determined to have the last word: "Shylock is our contemporary."

We all rise again when the Judges return. Their ruling is unanimous – according to Justice Ginsburg: the bond – the pound of flesh – is dismissed as a jest, one that no court in its right mind would grant; Antonio is ordered to repay his loan (though he is spared interest upon it); Shylock's fortune is restored; and his conversion revoked, on the grounds that Antonio, as defendant, had no right to demand it. What can I say? It is Shylock's lucky day.

The proceedings are rounded off with an invitation from Arrigo Cipriani – owner of Harry's Bar – to endless Bellinis in the vast hall downstairs. My father, long-since an expert in networking, is determined to secure an exchange with Justice Ginsburg. Tapping his glass against hers he says: "A Daniel come to judgment: yea a Daniel! O wise young judge how I do honour thee."

"Not so young," she says. My father quickly introduces himself, and proceeds to enlighten Justice Ginsburg as to the thesis of his famous book.

"Can you believe," he says, "that it was only in 2012 that Florida – of all places – struck the word 'shylock' from state statutes restricting usurious lending practices?"

"All too well," says Justice Ginsburg.

Whereupon my father reprises his Shylock equals Trump theory. The reference to Trump catches her off-guard.

"I can't imagine what the country would be with Donald Trump as our president," she says. "For the country it would be four years. For the court it could be – I don't even want to contemplate that."

I tug my father's sleeve. It is time to go to the Ghetto.

Maybe it's because we're tipsy, but we find our way with consumate ease. In the old days it was hard to get out of the Ghetto, tonight it's not so easy to get in. Squads of soldiers are stationed at its various entry points. They scrutinise our tickets and search our bags before granting us admission. Within other teams – armed to the teeth – patrol its two squares. In addition a permanent observation post has been established immediately before the Holocaust memorial, with its brick wall, barbed wire, and metal reliefs of humanity in extremis. Bleachers have been raised in the Campo del Ghetto Nuovo. Our seats are in the front row.

To my mind the most notable feature of the production, apart from its setting (which itself is enhanced by the fading of day into twilight, and the merging of twilight into night, whereupon the chorus of cicadas ceases its chirping), is the fact that Shylock's role is taken by five different actors (one of whom is actually an actress). For once the casting almost makes sense of Portia's question upon entering the courtroom, "Which is the merchant here, and which the Jew?", because we are not 100% sure ourselves.

Explanations for the multiple casting are provided in the

programme, by various members of the company: Compagnia de' Colombari. Its dramaturg, Walter Valeri, puts it this way: "We felt an almost 'natural' duty to commit dramaturgical heresy, to transfer Shylock into the body of five actors, make him slip out of his single, unique skin to underscore how each one of us is indeed Shylock."

Having read these sentences my father seems eager to punch Mr Valeri on the nose.

"What an idiot!" he says. "We don't go to the theatre to see ourselves mirrored on the stage, but to encounter a person with whom we can establish some sort of emotional contact; be it fear and loathing, affection, or pity. Shylock is our contemporary, but we are not Shylock. The pity we feel should be for him, not ourselves."

But, in truth, such an objection is to miss the point of the production. Its director – Karin Coonrod – does not invite her audience to feel, or to laugh very much, even though the play is nominally a comedy – but to think. And I'll tell you what gets me thinking. That scene when Tubal informs Shylock that his treacherous daughter – Jessica! – has traded a precious ring – stolen when she eloped with her Christian lover – for a monkey. Shylock is heart-broken. What else to call it?

"Thou torturest me, Tubal," he cries. "I had it of Leah when I was a bachelor. I would not have given it for a wilderness of monkeys."

If my father was upset when I told him that I would be studying Creative Writing at UEA, rather than English at USA, he did not show it. But the announcement did prompt him to pass on my mother's wedding ring.

"No pressure," he said, "but one day I hope to watch your husband slip it on to your finger under the chuppa."

For the last few weeks I have been trying to pluck up the courage to tell him that it will never happen, since my no-good boyfriend stole it to pay off his gambling debts. I begin to consider the absurd notion that my father already knows, and has brought me along to make me feel guilty.

The performance concludes, not with the traditional harmony in Belmont, but with each cast member repeating Shylock's challenge: "Are you answered?" Actually an answer of sorts does appear – like the writing on the wall – spread across several of the Ghetto's tenements: the Hebrew word, *Rahamim*, whose meaning is Mercy. I can only hope that my father will have mercy on me when he finally learns that the ring is lost.

****

We booked a round-trip on Easyjet.

For unannounced reasons the ground crew elects to board the return leg early, which means that we (who showed up at the gate at the appointed time) are among the last to embark. As it happens my meagre apparel is tucked into a back-pack, whereas my father is wheeling a small case. It's well within the prescribed limits, and had caused no comment on the outward flight, but this time he is informed that it will have to be placed in the hold rather than the over-head.

Without so much as a second thought my father says: "No. I've just heard that my wife is desperately ill, and I have to get home in a hurry."

"I'm sorry, sir," says one of the crew, "you have no choice."

"Don't you understand," says my father, "my wife may be dying, and I have to get home?"

I am rendered speechless by my father's betrayal. Where is the Prime Directive now? I'll tell you where: in tatters, on the floor of Marco Polo airport.

"There is nothing I can do for you," says the crew member, "you have to hand me your case."

"No, I don't," says my father, "and I won't."

Whereupon he walks straight out of the terminal and on to the waiting bus.

"Sir," says the crewman, "you have to come back here. I need to see your passport and your boarding card."

"I will not," says my father.

"If you do not," says the crewman, "I will have to contact the pilot, and he will have you thrown off the flight."

When I hear that I feel I have to intervene as the voice of reason. After all, I don't want to see my father gunned down as a suspected terrorist, which I explain would make him late in both senses of the word, and me an orphan.

****

Relations between us are correct but uncharacteristically tense after our return from Venice. Despite disavowals I assume that my father cannot fully repress his distress at watching me happily pack my belongings for a new life at UEA. For my part, I still cannot come to terms with his outrageous behaviour at the airport, which he has not even tried to explain. I only hope there is some sort of reconciliation before my departure.

I take it as evidence that my father feels the same, when he invites me to join him for a picnic on the University campus. It is one of those Indian summer days between Rosh Hashana and Yom Kippur, when the horse chestnuts slyly reveal their lustre, and the leaves are beginning to curl like burning paper. We decide to meet at Old Gorehambury House, the ruined mansion where the University's polymath patron saint, Sir Francis Bacon, once lived. We sit on the grass behind the unroofed house, and uncork a bottle of good red, but the conversation does not proceed as anticipated.

"Do you remember what killed your grandmother?" my father says.

"Of course," I say, "kidney disease."

"One of the first signs of kidney disease is blood in the urine," he says.

"Why are you telling me this?" I say.

"Because there was blood in mine when I went to pee in that restaurant where we dined with Shaul after my lecture," he says.

"My God," I yell, "why didn't you say something?"

"I didn't want to worry you," he says, "especially with you being so near the beginning of your university career."

"Was that the only episode?" I say.

"It happened again at the airport," he says, "which was why I was in such a hurry to get home."

"Why now?" I say. "Why are you telling me now?"

He pours me some wine.

"Drink up," he says.

"*L'Chaim*," I say.

"As you can imagine," he says, "I went straight to Dr Dow upon our return, my best hope being that I had contracted some sort of kidney infection from my dip in the canal. No such luck. When the blood work came back, Iain sent me straight for an ultrasound, which revealed the cause of my problem."

"Oh God, daddy," I say, leaning over and kissing him on the forehead.

"Now put two and two together," he says.

"You inherited the disease from your mother," I say.

"And?" he says.

"I might have inherited it from you," I say.

"Afraid so," he says, "it's a dominant gene, so there's a fifty-fifty chance. Even so, I still wasn't going to breath a word, given the likelihood that you won't have any symptoms for three decades or more."

"So what changed your mind?" I say.

"I'm starting dialysis next month," he says.

Before I can give voice to my response, a blond man trailed by an all-blond camera crew interrupts our conversation.

"Hallo," he says. "We are from Norway, and represent the Francis Bacon Society of Oslo. The purpose of our visit to St Albans is to make a little documentary about him. We understand that this is the house in which he secluded himself to pen the plays more usually attributed to Shakespeare. Are you able to confirm that we are in the right place?"

"Not only that," says my father, "but I can tell you that it was here – after his retirement in 1622 – where he saw through the press a selection of his plays still called the Shakespeare Folio. Careful reading, however, reveals the truth. On page 287 in *King Lear*, at the bottom of the second column, the endings unambiguously spell out: Sir-France-is-Bee-Con. You can check it out for yourselves. Bacon's own copy – recently discovered – is in Special Collections over there at New Gorehambury House."

The Norwegians stare at my father open-mouthed.

"Would you repeat that for the camera?" asks their leader.

My father does so with gusto, throwing in for good measure the preposterous notion that Bacon was the original author of Don Quixote, and Cervantes merely its Spanish translator.

"Give my regards to old Fortinbras," he says, as they depart.

"That was cruel," I say.

"They deserve it," he says. "The English are such snobs you can understand their difficulty in accepting that a lowly commoner could write the greatest plays ever conceived. But I always thought better of Scandinavians."

****

Without telling him I see Iain Dow, who agrees to refer me for an ultrasound at the City Hospital. It shows that I am my father's daughter. The cysts are evident, but a long way from threatening. There seems no reason not to tell my father the news. He hugs me and looks sufficiently upset, but I cannot help feeling that there is something shifty about his distress. Later I overhear him discussing the news with one of his cronies.

"Of course I had to appear devastated, and make no mistake: I was, for Jessica's sake at least," he says. "But if you can keep a secret, I need to make a confession."

Obviously the person at the other end of the line provides the necessary guarantees, because my father coughs, and recommences.

"The truth is, I also felt considerable relief," he says. "You remember the scene in the Merchant when that son-of-a-bitch

Salerio responds to Shylock's assertion that Jessica is his flesh and blood with taunts that query his paternity? 'There is more difference between thy flesh and hers,' says the antisemite mockingly, 'than between jet and ivory, more between your bloods, than there is between red wine and Rhenish'."

My father pauses, probably in response to a question.

"What has this to do with me?" he says. "I'll tell you. Around the time of Jessica's conception her mother grew very close to the Head of Drama at the college where she lectured. Leah always assured me that the relationship was entirely Platonic, and I had no evidence, let alone proof, that it was otherwise. But who needs proof when you've got suspicions? God forgive me, but I couldn't help but regard Jessica's ultrasound as a kind of paternity test."

I creep out of earshot. There's certain stuff about one's parents' lives that's better not to know.

At my father's invitation Professor Bassi comes to St Albans to deliver a summary of the quincentennial proceedings. It is mid-October, and my father is now a dialysand. We have dinner at home.

"Is there no way back," says Shaul, "no cure?"

"Only a transplant," says my father, "either cadaveric or altruistic, the latter usually from a close family member."

He laughs.

"How's this for irony?" he says. "My disease has turned me into a latter-day Shylock. He wanted a pound of flesh. I'd settle for a quarter. That's all a kidney weighs, you know."

I excuse myself early. Shaul wishes me God speed. On the morrow my father is driving me to Norwich. But before that happens I have a dream. In the dream my bedroom door opens quietly. A man enters. Moonlight illuminates a blade in his hand. Then his face. It is unmistakably that of Shylock. But Shylock is nothing without an actor, and on this occasion the actor is my father. He rolls me over roughly and prepares to plunge in the knife. I lie there trusting, awaiting the angel that will stay his hand. But this is no biblical dream. Nor does my father want to kill me, he merely wants my kidney, that little thing.

When I awaken I instinctively feel for the wound in my back, then laugh out loud when I touch only intact flesh. Relief courses through me like an adrenaline rush, not on account of the horror being nothing worse than a nighmare, but because I can suddenly see the advantages of the renal doctor's diagnosis. Polycystic Kidney Disease is my Portia, my guardian angel. Thanks to it I will never be in a position to donate that vital quarter pound of flesh to my father. Had my kidneys been unspeckled I would certainly have felt obligated to make the sacrifice, to toss him a lifebelt, as it were; something I would only have done with the greatest reluctance, if my dream is anything to go by. Now I can't, thank God. Obviously my father knew what he was doing when he called me Jessica.

As we part at Norwich I can see that my father is close to weeping. Turning to go he misquotes the last lines of the Merchant: "Well, while I live, I'll fear no other thing/ So sore, as keeping safe Jessica's ring." The words sting my eyes, but I blame the wind, which is blowing straight out of Russia.

Ain't That The Truth

DESPITE SHYLOCK'S FORCED conversion to Christianity, the joke was on Lorenzo, who had stolen his daughter. All four of his sons resembled his father-in-law. And so it continued down the line, *l'dor v'dor*. The more Lorenzo's descendants denied their Jewishness, the more Shylock's genes belied them. Many a horrible death was met on account of a nose.

No one knows who was the first of Shylock's heirs to emigrate to the United States, but a likely candidate is recorded as a resident of New York in the US census of 1860: Chaim Lokshen. By 1880 he had relocated to Deadwood, South Dakota, lured presumably by the prospect of gold. Though there were a few German immigrants there who pronounced his name correctly, most called him Chime, as in "Chimes at Midnight". Those who became his friends thought a diminutive necessary, and turned Chime to Chai. As Chaim assimilated more, so did his name, and he ended upbeing known to every one as Shy.

Thereafter the family slowly tracked the westward expansion of the United States, and by 1950 some of Shy Lokshen's descendants had settled in Las Vegas: Meyer and

Mimi Lokshen, plus their three daughters; Rosie, Becky, and Eva. A son, another Shy, was added in '57.

According to the records of Temple Beth Sholom, the last named celebrated his barmitzvah there in October 1970. It is also written that the sliding doors of the ark were opened by Moe Dalitz and one other. Dalitz also had the honour of lifting the Torah scroll from its resting place, and parading it around the packed interior, before young Shy took a deep breath and chanted his portion. A visitor might conclude that the only person in the entire building more Jewish than the Lokshens was the rabbi.

Moe Dalitz, whom Shy was encouraged to call Uncle Moe, was Meyer Lokshen's business associate. This connection lent young Shy a certain cachet at Greenfields High, an untouchability that transmitted itself even to his teachers. If anyone thought his nose risible, or his work inferior, they did not take the risk of saying so, at least to his face. When Shy inquired of his father about blood-curdling rumours that attached themselves to his Uncle's name, he was given a lecture on the taxonomical differences between gangsters and racketeers. Here it is in a nutshell.

"Gangsters," said Meyer, "cut throats, whereas racketeers merely cut corners."

"Okay," said Shy, "I buy the difference. But I still don't know how Uncle Moe makes his money."

"He runs rackets," said Meyer.

"Such as?" said Shy.

"Such as bootlegging and illegal betting," said Meyer. "Two enterprises that would make him a felon elsewhere, but just happen to be legal in the great state of Nevada."

"Lucky for him," said Shy.

"Lucky for us," said his father.

There was no denying that; the family lived in a grand house in Summerlin. It even had lawns with sprinklers.

"The most important thing to remember," his father added, "is that the Lokshens are no longer money lenders. It's our turn to borrow the stuff."

And the results were plain to see. In the late forties Meyer accumulated millions, from bank loans and insider trading, all of which he invested in Moe Dalitz's oases, speculative Xanadus such as the Stardust and the Desert Inn. Their flora and fauna were cards, dice, roulette wheels and showgirls. The interiors of these pleasure palaces were forbidden zones for young Shy, but he was permitted to attend the numerous pool parties hosted by Uncle Moe's vivacious daughter. Cousin Suzanne was also off-limits, but her friends were a different matter, and with them Shy was anything but. It's true that he didn't have the looks to match his bravado, but money and connections count in Vegas. There was a time when I dated a girl Shy had just dumped. Surprisingly she wasn't bitter. I understood why when she showed me the bracelet he had given her as a parting gift.

My family couldn't afford Summerlin, but I did attend Greenfields High, where I was Shy's only competition in Mr Hunter's class on rhetoric. We also played together on the soccer team; Shy in the front line, me watching his back in goal. Though we never became close friends, we did develop a certain rapport. It went nowhere after graduation, however, because Shy was accepted at Harvard's Business School, whereas I had to settle for a degree in Jurisprudence from the University of Nevada. When I returned to Sin City I joined the LVPD, one of very few Jews to do so. As my lieutenant liked to say: "It takes one to catch one."

Maybe it was the lack of sunlight in the East, but when

Shy came home with his MA from Harvard, he looked a changed man. What was left of his hair was lank and greasy. His complexion was bookishly grey. Every time he shrugged his shoulders he seemed to shrink a little more. How shall I put it? He was no longer Shy, he was Shylock full-blown. No sooner had he resettled in Vegas, than first Mimi, then Meyer, died in quick succession. By that time Rosie, Becky and Eva were all married; one to an orthodontist, another to an ophthalmic surgeon, and the third to a dog groomer. Meantime their little brother was dating an exotic dancer, who called herself Lady Macbeth. She was the only stripper in the Pair-a-Dice without a single tattoo on her body. Upon meeting her parents Shy found out why. They announced themselves as Holocaust survivors. In fact both had been born in separate suburbs of Chicago, but had they not been (they argued), had they been born in the Old Country, they would certainly have been murdered by the Nazis. Shy said he understood their logic.

"When you think of it like that," he added, "all Jews are survivors."

After Shy became a multi-millionaire on the death of his father, Lady Macbeth was happy to hang up her G-string, and accept his proposal that she become Mrs Lokshen. She immediately commenced her life's work of restocking the planet with Jews.

Shy, orphaned at twenty-four, and already a father at twenty-five, decided it was time for his family to take their rightful place centre stage. No longer would the Lokshens be the sleeping partner, but the ones to deal with. It helped that by then Uncle Moe had stepped back from the business, thus rendering redundant any whisperings on his wife's part in praise of regicide. Learning of Shy's ambitions to build a new casino on the Strip, the Mob decided to muscle in, with offers of favourable loans, guaranteed co-operation from the city's public works director, not to mention the unions, and a complete protection package.

"It's a real sweetheart deal," said Tony Francisco, "only a fool would turn his back on it."

In those years, at least, Shy was no fool: he knew that a degree, even one from an ivy-league college, cut no ice in the desert; he also understood that it was too early in his career to antagonize the Mob.

As the two men shook hands, Tony Francisco said: "Of course, if you don't pay the premiums we'll be forced to take our pound of flesh, first from your beautiful wife, next from you, and finally from your delightful daughter. But this is just the small print. It will never come to that."

That was back in '82.

As the years passed I transferred to the Vice Squad, and listened as one Federal Investigator after another boasted that they were going to nail Shy Lokshen for corruption of government officials. But none ever did. Shy beat every one, and all the while built bigger and bigger casinos. There were rumours that we had become too close – I'll take the Fifth on that – but the truth is that I did agree to become the in-house detective at his newest and grandest venture, the Doge's Palace.

It rose from the desert with no distinguishing features, but oh the interior. Within was a miraculous landscape of renaissance squares and full-size canals. These internal waterways were more than whimsy. To bring them to life a fleet of gondolas had been imported from Venice, as well as their sweet-voiced pilots. Blue skies replaced ceilings. The cloudscape above St Mark's Square was pitched at twilight, at the permanent cocktail hour, permitting guests to guiltlessly sip their favourite spirit mix whatever the real time. The Palace's foundations were great gambling halls, fine examples of 21st-century Americana, but connecting them were colonnaded corridors, and frescoed ceilings from which hung magnificently wrought lamps and chandeliers, illuminating more scenes of classical frivolity on the walls, and a marble walk-way with trompe-l'oeil designs that created steps where none were. On the seventy-five other floors, there were forty restaurants and bars, six swimming pools, and more rooms than I could count. This was Venice reimagined as a vertical city. Only the exterior campanile – a full-size replica of the original – looked incongruous, being surrounded by automobiles. There was another difference: it sounds absurd, given the number of people sleeping in those rooms, but it felt like a space devoid of dreams, by which I mean the sort of dreams that might interest Sigmund Freud.

But of avarice there were plenty. And Shy knew how to exploit those better than most. I think I got the clearest insight into why he built the Doge's Palace late one afternoon, when we wandered through its newly opened casino, with its low ceilings, card tables, roulette wheels, and row after row of solitary stools placed before a gaudy phalanx of armour-plated slot machines.

"If my hotel were truly Venice," he said, "then this area would be its ghetto. Our enemies claim that we Jews are only interested in making money, and cite our long history of usury. But, given the many attractions of the Doge's Palace, which one do the goyim favour above all others? They spat on my ancestor for charging interest. But look at them. Just look at them. They still expect money for nothing. The suckers!"

Shy's Venice may have been a city without a memory, but obviously his was intergenerational.

Amid all its stores dedicated to the sale of sportswear, high fashion, and electrical goods, just one stood out: a rare book dealer of some repute. In its windows alongside first editions of *Moby Dick*, *Huckleberry Finn*, and *The Great Gatsby* was an original copy of Israel's Declaration of Independence, priced at $15000. What wasn't on display was a book the store's owners had acquired, not so much to sell, but to take out of circulation: Henry Ford's own copy of the *Protocols of the Elders of Zion*. They gifted it to Shy who showed it to his wife.

"Why would I want such filth?" she said.

"Sorry," said her husband, reaching for the offending item.

"Not so fast," said Mrs Lokshen. "Let me take a look. Maybe world domination isn't such a bad idea if it guarantees our people's safety."

"When you put it like that," said Shy, "it doesn't sound so crazy."

He had grown sick of turning the other cheek, of habitually kowtowing to Tony Francisco and the Mob.

That night, in their Summerlin retreat, Mrs Lokshen gave her husband a précis.

"According to the Protocols, the quickest route to world domination is through subverting the morals and morale of the goyim," she said. "We're already doing a pretty good job of the former with our casinos. The latter requires us to seize control of the world's economy and its press. Where shall we start?"

"Where else," said her husband, "but Jerusalem?"

Looking at the available politicians, Shy selected Bobo

Sobol, leader of the Likud party. With elections approaching Shy founded a free newspaper, whose only function was to persuade the voters of Bobo Sobol's pre-eminent suitability for the post of prime minister, which he duly became. A few well-placed, and well-timed bombs, purportedly placed by the enemy, did nothing to hinder his irresistible rise.

"Tell him to expand the settlements," said Mrs Lokshen, "tell him to annex Judea and Samaria."

"The Americans won't let him do that," said Shy.

"Okay," said Mrs Lokshen, "now we know what our next task is."

That's when I got involved.

One day Shy asked me to drive him over to Death Valley.

"We'll need the four-by-four," he said.

We left early, hitting the I-95 before dawn. Even so the temperature was 109 in the shade by the time we arrived. And there was no shade. Somewhere between Zabriskie Point and Scottie's Castle, we turned off the black-top on to a dirt road. Approximately five miles down was a wooden shack. Shy ordered me to pull over.

"I want to let you in on a secret," he said. "I'm building a golem."

"A golem?" I said. "I'm no expert, but wasn't it associated with Prague rather than Venice?"

"It's not for the new place," Shy said.

"Where then?" I said.

"The White House," he said.

It didn't happen in a day, but together we fashioned a man out of the sands of Death Valley, assisted by a latter-day Michaelangelo, slumming as a prop-maker at the Doge's Palace.

"Aren't you worried he'll spill the beans?" I said.

"No," said Shy.

I convinced myself that his silence had been bought with an outsize payment.

The golem's flesh tones were of an unnatural hue, but could certainly pass for human in Las Vegas, and likely elsewhere too. His face, however, required a few more humanizing touches. Instead of tendering for false teeth, Shy gave the job direct to his brother-in-law, preferring to keep this part of the intrigue within the family. In a matter of days the golem had a dazzling set of dentures. Another brother-in-law fitted glass eye-balls, with seductive brown irises. And the third, the dog-groomer, fashioned a louche toupée from the clippings left behind by an Afghan hound. When fitted a kiss curl fell conveniently over the word *emet* – meaning "truth" – necessarily impressed upon the golem's forehead. The next stage, of course,was to breathe life into it, to turn it from a thing into a being. As a lawman I had been instructed in CPR, but felt that in this instance my skills were way off the mark.

"What next?" I said, as we stood before the inanimate giant.

"Funny you should ask," said Shy. "As you know my cabarets are the finest in Vegas. Especially the magicians. Once in every generation the real thing shows up; a man who can turn water to wine. Such a miracle-worker is presently topping the bill at one of my smaller casinos. When I propositioned him he asked for more time. Well, time's up. Bring him here, whatever he says."

And that's exactly what I did, despite his threats to turn me into a toad. Had I known what he was capable of I would likely have told Shy I couldn't find him, but I hadn't yet seen him animate a handful of sand. It turned out that he was pretty good at disappearing too, though whether Shy had any part in that I chose not to ask.

The golem was privately educated. He lived on the top floor of the Doge's Palace. For a year it marked the limits of his world. The first outsider he met was Tony Francisco. Tony Francisco left the Doge's Palace on a stretcher. Shy looked pleased with the handiwork of his protégé, though he knew no golem came without caveats.

"According to legend," said Shy, "a golem has irony in its DNA. Built to save, it ends up threatening to destroy. It also has a tendency to run amok. Should that happen it's your job to terminate him."

"You mean with this?" I said, indicating my service revolver.

"You crazy?" said Shy. "The thing's supernatural. A monster. You think bullets will stop him?"

"So what will?" I said.

"Magic," said Shy. "Rub out the first 'e' on his forehead, so that you're left with *met*, which means 'death'. That always stops them in their tracks, or so I've read."

By then we had a pretty good idea of the golem's character; he was boastful, cruel, incurious, merciless, and of course he lacked a soul. It was nearing the time to introduce him to a wider audience. But how? In what profession would such deficiencies serve as assets? Shy asked his wife if she had any suggestions.

"Isn't boxing called the Noble Art?" she said.

The golem stood six six in his socks, and weighed in at 230lbs of muscle and bone. His blood pressure was an enviable 120/70, and his heart rate was fixed at 72 bpm. We decided to give him a sex drive, but argued over how strong it should be. I suggested sluggish, for fear of scandals, but Shy was adamant.

"We've created a man of towering ambition, not a shrinking violet," he said. "He needs his full whack of testosterone, to feed it, and a dick to match."

Within months of becoming a boxer, the golem was a serious contender. Shy arranged to stage the title fight at the Teatro La Fenice, not the one in Venice, but its exact replica which sat in the heart of the Doge's Palace. The champion – the first boxer of Italian descent to hold the title since Rocky Marciano – was the bookies' favourite, and the crowd's darling. Shy, on the other hand, saw the bout in terms of a belated rematch: Antonio, Bassanio, Lorenzo – take your pick – versus his distant ancestor. The place was packed, every seat sold. Luckily for me the LVPD were present in force to assist my small team. The bell rang for round one. The golem landed blow after blow. Sweat sprang from his opponent's brow, and shone in the spotlight like a star-spangled banner. The bout ended in the fourth with a knock-out. The golem's opponent was in a coma for a month.

"He only broke my jaw," Tony Francisco was heard to boast.

"The conquest of America began tonight" said Shy, as we locked the theatre.

In the months that followed the golem saw off a series of challengers – a fellow American, a Russian, a Cuban, and a Nigerian – all of whom suffered the same humiliating fate: lights out by the fifth. The golem started dating a super-model. When asked what she saw in him, the golem interjected: "What's not to see in me? I'm the Marlbro Man of erections. If I fuck her on Sunday she's still coming on Wednesday." Other women attested that this was no idle boast. At first Shy despaired of such talk, fearing it would ruin the golem's reputation, but he soon saw that it actually enhanced it.

After that time, the golem became a darling of the talk shows. He didn't say much, but he didn't have to after Jimmy Fallow took a swing at his chin and broke his hand. Instead of offering to kiss it better, the golem stormed off the set, saying, "I don't talk to losers." The phrase went viral. It was, after all, the perfect way to break off any uncomfortable conversation.

He used the phrase to even better effect during the Town Hall debates to select a Republican candidate, once Shy had decided the time was ripe for a Presidential bid. Among other things this meant commissioning professionals to sell the golem to the American people. After reviewing the pitches of several agencies, Shy had selected one of the big boys, whose HQ was on Madison Avenue: Y&R, no less. A hotshot copywriter was immediately dispatched from NYC. The golem's firm handshake created a strong first impression.

"It's both warm and dry," the copywriter said, as if that were already a desirable political position.

Having checked into the Doge's Palace he sequestered himself and eventually emerged with a number of strap-lines. He summoned his new clients to one of the hotel's many conference centres and declaimed his efforts.

"Not bad," said Shy, "not bad at all."

The golem appeared less impressed, though how he expressed that dissatisfaction I'm not entirely sure, since he chose to remain silent. But the copywriter was one of those world-weary types; he knew dissatisfaction when he saw it. So he tried harder.

"America used to be top dog," he said. "Together we can be again."

"NO!" said the golem. "Follow me and we will be again."

That's when we realized that the golem had begun to develop a mind of his own.

Unlike his rivals the golem was not peddling policies in the manner of a door-to-door salesman. The niceties of such things were not for him. He did not argue with his competitors over how many redwoods to preserve in the Californian forests, or whether there was a distinction between infanticide and abortion, he simply exposed and exploited his opponents' weak spots, making them appear ineffectual and ridiculous. One after another they dropped out of the race. Come the Convention he was the only candidate left standing, and was chosen by acclaim. His Democratic opponent probably breathed a sigh of relief, thinking him unelectable. But she also had her problems. People like Mrs Lokshen hated her beyond all reason, and were prepared to believe the very worst of her. An acquaintance of Shy's claimed to have been told by an acquaintance of his, that the candidate had been heard to whisper in the ear of an advisor: "The world would be a better place without Israel."

"It's the same old story," said Shy. "No one wants us around. Then they cry after we're gone. Only this time we ain't going."

Through his puppet in Jerusalem he pressed the Democratic candidate to declare her limitless support for the State of Israel, which of course she did. But that was not sufficient for Shy. The last of the Presidential Debates was scheduled at a rival casino on the Strip. Somehow he managed to ensure that a question was asked on the status of Jerusalem and the legality of the settlements. Both candidates agreed on the fact that Jerusalem undivided was Israel's eternal capital, but when the Democratic candidate denounced the settlements as impediments to peace, the golem simply rolled his big brown eyes and gave a Heil Hitler salute behind her back.

Obviously Shy didn't know this at the time, but the gesture also served as a covert signal of support to the golem's other constituency: the Ku Klux Klan, whose Grand Wizards recognised no contradiction between their inherent antisemitism and their support for Israel. It was simply a matter of their enemy's enemy being their friend. The common enemy, as they saw it, being Islam. Moreover, the average Klansman just adored his unapologetic catch-phrase, and his total disregard for political etiquette. They saw in him – or so they thought – one of their own. As a matter of fact they were wrong; the golem did not share their ideology: neither political philosophy nor politics itself meant anything to him. All he cared about was acclaim, and ratings.

Remembering the importance of controlling the press, Shy acquired the *Las Vegas Sentinel*, but failed in his attempts to purchase *The New York Times*, the LA Times, and *The Washington Post*. But it probably didn't matter; their readers were unlikely to become golem voters, however compelling the arguments put forth. But for rednecks the golem was the chosen one. Though incapable of love, it seems he could inspire it in others. He wasn't just any golem, but the undisputed heavyweight champion of the world. People started to call him "Champ". And that's what he became: their champion. How else to explain his improbable victory on election night. They likely thought he would take out the bad guys on their behalf. Oh the excitement in the Doge's Palace as first Indiana, then – in rapid succession – Illinois, Wisconsin, Iowa, Michigan and finally Florida, all fell to the golem. Shy might not have bought the NYT, but he had manufactured the next President of the United States. Out of gratitude the golem offered to marry his daughter and make her First Lady.

"Well Jessica?" said Shy. "It's a good offer."

"I need time," said Jessica.

She was in love with a comedian playing at a dive way off the Strip who did golem impressions.

"Why not marry the real thing?" said her mother, when Jessica gave up the reason for her hesitation.

The next time they met the comedian had some news for Jessica: "My agent has just received this incredible offer from Macao. So much money. I'd be a lunatic not to take it."

It was probably no coincidence that Shy had a controlling interest in Macao's largest casino.

Out of pique Jessica agreed to become Mrs President.

"For a couple of rookie conspirators we're not doing so badly," said Mrs Lokshen. "First we took Jeruslem, and now Washington does our bidding."

Or so it seemed.

On the eve of the inauguration Shy felt it necessary to remind the golem of his *raison d'être*.

"You were created for a single purpose," he said, "to protect the Jewish people. Whether you are one yourself is for wiser heads to decide. Either way, it has no effect on your mission. Everywhere we are under siege, nowhere more so than in our beloved homeland. Now that a miracle has occurred, and you have actually become President of the United States, you must forget the oath of office. Your first duty will not be to the Constitution, or to the American people, who can take care of themselves on the whole, but to *Am Yisroel*, to the people of Israel and the Jews worldwide, who bleed continuously. Do you understand? Above all this requires Israel to be as strong as possible. Once in office you must end all talk about a Palestinian state, move our embassy to Jerusalem, and recognize the legality of all the settlements. Then, for the first time in two thousand years, we may actually feel safe. The world owes us that much."

For the inauguration itself the bride-to-be wore a black Giorgio Armani wrap with an astrakhan collar. And she needed it; an icy wind was blowing flakes of snow up the Mall. It toyed with the golem's kiss curl, partially revealing the Hebrew lettering on his forehead, which were interpreted by the clear-sighted as worry lines. Of course he eschewed a coat when he took the oath of office, and made his inaugural speech, which Shy had written, and I had endeavoured to make as uncontentious as possible. But I couldn't get him to budge on moving the embassy to Jerusalem that very month.

"You want to start the third intifada?" I argued.

"Would it be such a bad thing?" said Shy. "At least the world will get to see the Palestinians in their true colours."

When the embassy was transferred, the response was as predicted: stone-throwing and worse from Temple Mount, and the resumption of suicide bombings in markets and on buses. Fifty dead within a week. Bobo Sobol's punishment was harsh; not only were the families of the bombers expelled, but entire villages too. The UN howled, but the President of the United States said nothing. What were displaced people to him, when evangelicals wept in his presence, and thanked him for bringing Armageddon that much closer?

Given the upheaval in Israel and the Occupied Territories, I was astonished to hear how the golem intended to reward Bobo Sobol on his forthcoming visit to Washington. Even Shy went a little pale. The Skype connection was good, so there was no possibility of a misunderstanding.

"I intend to declare my country's go-ahead for building the Third Temple on Temple Mount, where it belongs," said the voice from the capital. "Let's be fair, the Muslims already have two beautiful mosques up there, so why not a Temple for the Jews? After all, it is their most holy site. And, if my advisers are correct, only number three for the Muslims."

"Advisers? What advisers?" said Shy.

"Good men," said the golem. "Evangelicals from the West, Klansmen from the South."

The sort of men who want to bring down the old order, and provoke a world-wide conflict between the Christian west and the Muslim east, with Jerusalem as the fire-starter.

We drove out to the desert, where no one else could hear us, and discussed the consequences of such a pledge.

"Look, Shy," I said, as our shadows lengthened, "I was a cop and I know the laws of cause and effect. You hit me, and I'll hit you back harder. If the golem makes good on his promise, the conflict won't stay local for long. Iran will get involved for sure, which means that the Saudis will feel obliged to pitch in with a higher bid."

"You know policing, I know poker," said Shy, "the Saudis will be bluffing."

"Maybe so," I said, "but I'd bet my house that the Iranians won't be. If they have nuclear weapons – a possibility you have been warning the world about for years – they are just meshugge enough to use them. Let's suppose they launch six, and that the Israelis take down five."

"God forbid even one gets through," said Shy. "Either way, America is certain to intervene on Israel's behalf, by which time Israel would have flattened Tehran."

"Then what?" I said.

"No doubt you are going to tell me," said Shy.

"However much the Saudis might hate the Iranians, they are fellow Muslims," I said, "and would feel compelled to form an alliance, which all the other Arab countries would join. Europe will try to remain neutral, of course, but there are just too many Islamic State sleeper cells. Boom goes Berlin! Boom goes Paree! Who will be the first to take the nuclear option is anybody's guess. Maybe it will be our own President. In any event, what we are looking at is an imminent Armageddon. Rapture for the Evangelicals, maybe, but curtains for the rest of us. And who will inherit the earth after we're gone? The golem, of course. For sure, he'll be baked a little harder, and his complexion will be a little more tan, but he will be lord of all he surveys. His only subjects? A diaspora of cockroaches. Was that really what you had in mind when you created him? Let the golem carry on and you'll be responsible for loving Israel to death."

"I think you are forgetting yourself, my friend," said Shy. "You are not Henry Kissinger. You are nothing but a washed-up ex-cop turned house detective at a Las Vegas hotel. My Las Vegas hotel. Do you seriously think it's part of your job description to tell me how to run the world's affairs?"

"Didn't you once warn me that one day you might lose control of the golem? Maybe just maybe – that day has come."

Like the day, Shy cooled down.

"So we have to silence him before Bobo Sobol arrives next week," said Shy. "We could send out Jessica. She was looking forward to the wedding, but not the marriage."

"Nah," I said, "it's an odious club to join: the Presidential Assassins. I'll go. But I need an accomplice."

"Name him," said Shy.

"Your brother-in-law, the dog groomer," I said.

We stood and hugged on the desert's shifting sands,

watching the sky drape itself in black, as the day bled out.

Needless to say, I told the dog groomer nothing about the nature of our mission, except to say that the golem's toupée needed some fine-tuning.

We took a taxi to the White House. At the gate was the primary injunction: Do Not Enter; and below a subsidiary: Report to Security Official. We sought out the gatekeeper, as instructed, and accidentally violated an invisible red line. But the Official's station was empty, so we turned around. As we did so the blue door of the porter potty – adjacent to the booth – swung open and a giant, like the golem, but with darker skin tones, emerged.

"Hey," he shouted, striding up the path towards us, "what you doing here?"

He was at least six-five; out of shape, but unquestionably intimidating. There was something of the bear about him; amiable in appearance, but at the same time unpredictable, and potentially dangerous. He was uniformed, and armed, though only with a handgun and a nine-inch Bowie knife sticking out of his belt. According to the tag stitched to his military-style shirt his name was "Gobbo".

"Where you people come from?" he said. "Not from around here?"

"From the other side," we said. "Nevada."

"I take it they teach you to read English in that Godforsaken state," he said.

He led us back, over the invisible boundary we had unwittingly transgressed, and positioned himself before the most prominent of the signs.

"Now take another look at that notice and tell me what it says," he said. "It says 'Do Not Enter'. I assume you know what those words mean. They mean 'Do-Not-Enter'. And what did you go and do? You went and entered anyway. From my point of view that makes you either stupid or a criminal."

"But the sign also has a sub-heading," I said. "It advises visitors to report to the attendant, and that is what we were trying to do. We were looking for you. Besides which we have an appointment to see the President."

"It's not your job to look for me," said Gobbo. "Your job is to obey the sign. Your job is to stand right here and not move. Remember what the sign says. It says: 'Do-Not-Enter'. So you do not enter. When I see you I'll come to you and find out what you want."

"But you couldn't see us," said Shy's brother-in-law, "you were in the porter potty. That's why we came looking."

"It doesn't matter where I was," said Gobbo. "It was your job to wait for me to find you."

"Now you have found us," I said, "can we enter?"

"Nobody can come in," said Gobbo. "That's the point. That's why the sign says: 'Do Not Enter'. That's why I am here: to stop you entering."

His hand moved, perhaps unconsciously, to the handle of his pistol.

"Okay," I said, "can you inform some figure of authority that we are here, so that he can come and fetch us."

"Me doing my duty is nothing to smile about," said Gobbo. "I don't think you'd think it so funny if I exercised my right to arrest the both of you, which I am entitled to do. See this shoulder patch? To whom, in the final analysis, am I answerable?"

"I used to be a cop myself," I said, "I know the score."

"Just answer my question," he said.

"The President," I said.

"Exactly," he said. "The President is our boss of bosses; though he remains answerable to the people and the law. Now explain what you want with him."

My problem was that while I had in my possession a letter inviting us to attend upon the President, it also instructed us to show it to no one, because the President, always vain, did not want anyone to know that his toupée was attended to by a dog groomer.

"We've come to talk business," I said. "Phone ahead to check that our names are on the visitor's list. We can wait."

"You bet you can," he said, making no move to pick up the phone. "Tell me, are you two illiterates Jews? You look like Jews to me. There's something about you I don't trust. Why don't I trust Jews? Because the Jews invented banking, that's why. The whole American banking system is based on the model they built. It looks solid, but the stock market is what? I'll tell you; it's one giant casino. And who loses? I'll give you a clue. The house always wins. It's thanks to the banks and their ways that we have regular crises built into the system. You want to know the truth about it? Read *Web of Debt* by Ellen Hodgson Brown. Here's another unpalatable truth for you white folks to digest. If it wasn't for the black man America might still be part of the British Empire. But God had a plan. He put us here for a reason. To pick cotton. The black man picking cotton paid for the war that won America's freedom from England. Now – thanks to the black man – the sun never sets on the American empire."

"We may look like Jews," I said, "but we ain't. We're spies. Our assignment? To work undercover. To learn just how the Shylocks are cooking the books. And we're here to report our findings direct to the President. When he's done listening I can guarantee you one thing: the black man will get a fair shake of the dice."

"Why didn't you say so in the first place?" said Gobbo.

On learning that we did indeed have security clearance he signed us in, and waved us through.

We found the golem pacing around the Oval Office in some distress.

"Why aren't my ratings better?" he wailed. "I've given the people what they want. Why don't they love me right back?"

"Take a seat and let Shy's brother-in-law see to your hairpiece," I said. "That'll calm you down."

"My advisers maintain that there is no such thing as a fact," said the golem, "and that truth lies in the eye of the beholder. They say: 'Fiction produces results when facts fail.' They tell me: 'It's not what you did. It's what people believe you did or will do. Everything is relative.' What do you say to that?"

I said: "Bullshit. I'm an ex-cop, not a philosopher, and if I didn't have a basic idea of what truth is, if I thought I had sent an innocent man to jail, I would not be able to live with myself."

"That's all very well," said the golem, "but how do you know when someone is telling a lie? Maybe you think them innocent because they are great actors? Or guilty simply because they fail to convince."

"Good cops look for evidence," I said. "But what if they can't find any?" he said. "They look harder," I said. But I'm obviously a hopeless actor, because I couldn't budge the golem from his belief that everything was just a matter of opinion, that there was no such thing as truth. "Maybe you'd like to see a little demonstration of its power?" I said.

He just laughed. I admit that I felt pretty bad about what I was about to do, until I reminded myself that the golem wasn't human. Having squared things with my conscience, I ordered the dog groomer to brush back the kiss curl, and with dexterity that surprised me, erased the first letter on the golem's forehead; turning *emet* to *met*. The effect was immediate.

"Oh my God!" said Shy's brother-in-law. "You've killed the President." "Ain't that the truth," I said.

Shylock's Ghost

MY SON, THE movie director, has flown over from LA to shoot a reboot of *The Merchant of Venice*, at locations in Golders Green and Kenwood. The title has been adjusted accordingly, needless to say. How many times do I get to see my son? Not often enough, now that we inhabit different continents. I haunt the sets. There are long lines of white trucks, each truck with its own transformative power; the ability to turn night to day, for example, and ordinary human beings into immortals of the silver screen. And above them all, like some latter-day Zeus, sits my son. I do not like to interrupt him at work, so I take the opportunity to revisit my childhood in nearby Hendon; a melancholy business, given that I am its only survivor. Hendon is but two stops from Golders Green on the Northern Line. Emerging from the underground I immediately spot that the Gaumont has become a gym called Virgin Active, and that WH Smith, my emporium of extra-curricular reading, has been swallowed by the adjacent Nat West. Turning left down Queen's Road I note that the Sydney Francis School of Dancing, where some poor woman did her best to teach me how to waltz and foxtrot in preparation for my barmitzvah party, is another absentee. And where oh where is Wittakers, retailers of Dinky toys and Meccano sets? I continue along Queen's Road, almost to its very end, seeking out the location of the Crest, my first school. As it happens, the building, a large suburban semi-detached, is still there, but the institution is long gone. Across the road is the flat green expanse of Hendon Park, where we were often let loose at playtime. I have no recollection of what we got up to in the park, as a rule, but I do well remember the occasion when we were hurried back to school, even before we had – as always instructed – looked both ways. On the far side, among the shrubs, a uniformed constable was wrestling with a miscreant, like Jacob with the Angel. We watched in fascination as they rolled over the dry earth, before our teacher was able to shield us from this vision of the real world.

To my astonishment, when I take a second look, I see that the fight is continuing, as though part of a perpetual lesson. It takes a few more moments to register that the opponents are actually different: one is wearing some sort of a costume – long black gown, long black pantaloons, and a red three-cornered hat – that clearly marks him out as a Jew; while the other is some category of antisemite. If the semiotics of his clothing, haircut and tattoos are not sufficient to identify him as such, his yells leave no room for doubt: "Take that you fucking Jewish cunt!" is one. To his evident surprise the fucking Jew receives his blow, and repays it with interest. That being the case, my intervention is not strictly necessary, but I can hardly turn my back on a co-religionist in trouble. Outnumbered and outfought the belligerent goy exits from the drama, having served his purpose.

"The joke is on him," says the victor, brushing soil from his outlandish costume, "I am not in fact a member of the unforeskinned race, though I am pleased to be mistook for one. That being the purpose of this outing: to test my costume and complexion, which is much lighter when I am out of costume, as befits a bold son of Eireann. The results have been most gratifying. Allow me to introduce myself," he continues, holding out his hand. "Charles Macklin, out of County Donegal, a hard drinker, a general lover, great bruiser, and an actor of high regard."

"A method actor, I presume?" I say.

"I know not what that might be," he says, "except that there is surely method in my madness."

That's when it occurs to me that he must be the actor cast as Shylock in my son's magnum opus.

Right character, wrong production.

It turns out that Mr Macklin is seeking Hendon Hall, a colonnaded mansion in the classical style, now a hotel, offering temporary sanctuary to my son and his crew, but formerly home to Sir David Garrick, the great actor-manager of the Georgian age.

"I am looking," says Macklin, "to bow the knee to the new king of Drury Lane, and thereafter persuade him to commence his reign at the Theatre Royal with my lauded impersonation of the most famous Jew outside the Old Testament."

Out of curiosity I offer to be a guide to this deluded thespian, perhaps on day release from one of the local loony bins. So what to make of the fact that, at the end of our hike along Brent and Parson Streets, then Ashley Lane, we are announced by a servant in full livery, and finally greeted by a man who introduces himself as Sir David Garrick? Surely I am dreaming? We are invited to take our seats in padded armchairs.

"Your majesty," says Macklin, "I am not interested in playing Shylock as a comic buffoon, as is the custom nowadays, but as Shakespeare writ him, as a vengeful daemon. This was how I presented him six years ago, during the prior era at Drury Lane, when it was said that my performance so terrified George II that he was robbed of sleep for a week."

"Contracts will be drawn up," says Garrick, with a smile. "I have already heard it whispered that the announcement of Macklin as Shylock sounds as attractive on the playbill as Garrick in Hamlet."

Macklin exits the Hall a happy man. Having secured the role, he wonders where he may obtain a pound of flesh, so that he may know properly what he is demanding. If there is a Garrick still in Hendon Hall, I think, there is every chance of finding Leslie Mann – family butchers – in Vivian Avenue. So we retrace our steps to Hendon Central – where the Gaumont is showing *Shane*, and WH Smith Booksellers has magically reappeared. Vivian Avenue too is the Vivian Avenue of yesteryear. As well as Leslie Mann, there is Martin's, the grocer; Graber's the delicatessen; Carmelli, the Israeli fruitier, with exotics such as pink grapefruit, persimmon and pomegranates on display; and finally Grodzinski, with its strong aroma of baking bread.

Standing outside Leslie Mann, Macklin asks: "What does 'kosher' mean?"

"That the animals are slaughtered in a particular way," I say, "and their flesh drained of blood."

"Not a drop remaining?" he says.

"Not a drop."

"Portia would approve," says he.

I emerge from the shop with a pound of anaemic mince.

With the meat as an offering we proceed to the end of Vivian Avenue, turn right into Station Road, and before I know it we are standing before my parents' house, exactly as it was when I last saw it. Out of habit I dig my hand into my pocket and, incredibly, feel the distinctive front-door key within. It still fits in the lock.

"I'm home," I shout, as I always do.

Following me Macklin decides to reinhabit the role of Shylock, perhaps to see if he can pass amongst Jews.

"Mrs Salmon," he says, on being introduced to my mother, "forgive my emotion, but your looks put me in mind of my lost daughter."

My mother blushes and says it is her sister, not she, who is the family beauty, but she is clearly charmed.

"You must stay for dinner," she says.

"Only if you will allow me to provide the main course," says Macklin.

At first my mother hesitates, but as soon as she sees its provenance she relaxes. Over dinner she rehearses an ancient bone of contention – the destination of our next summer holiday – looking to our renowned guest for reinforcement.

"For goodness sake," she says, "if you don't make up your mind soon we'll end up in Bournemouth. Are we going to Venice, or are we not?"

"I'm waiting on the payment of some overdue debts," says my father. "If the money comes through, we'll be on our way."

"Look what I have to put up with," she says. "It is a great pity Mr Salmon is not more like you, Mr Shylock. But he is too soft, like a two-minute egg. And he forgives his debtors too easily."

If this is a dream, it is not a healthy one: I feel as though trapped in a ghost story. I decide to return to the real world, where the actor playing Shylock is not two centuries old. I make my excuses, and kiss my parents goodbye. It is like kissing clouds. I return to Golders Green, and follow the orange arrows to the film set. My son is directing the trial scene. I do not want to disturb his concentration, but I cannot resist blowing him a kiss. A gesture he elects to ignore. Indeed, rather than acknowledge my presence, he looks right through me, as if I were as insubstantial as a kodachrome.